October Nights 2

Also by James B. Christensen

Honeymoon Phase

The Vessel

October Nights

October Nights 2

James B. Christensen

ISBN: 978-0-578-41039-5 (Ravensbook)

For Dad, who walks with the angels, and Mom, who carries on.

CONTENTS

Silver Hollow

Pole Thompson rode into Silver Hollow by moonlight. He had given thought to one more night of camping on the plains, but the fall chill quickly gave way to a blustery winter bite. He already passed through some snow on his way north. Tonight he wanted a warm meal in his belly and a mattress under his back. His horse, Tula, was sprightly and up for a few more hours of travel, so he continued on.

Pole kept his eyes moving, scanning the horizon in the silver light. He had that being-watched feeling. Many gunfights in many mining camps and timber towns had honed his sixth sense of survival. Tula snorted and shook her bridle.

"You sense it too, girl?" Pole asked, patting the animal's neck.

Skittering sounds among distant boulders sounded to his left. Pole pulled Tula to a halt. His gun was already out and aimed. Nothing other than the howl of the wind.

"Lots of night animals out," he said. "We were warned."

He was warned, but the money he'd been offered was good. Real good. Retire to San Francisco with any woman he wanted good. The assignment he had to complete for the payoff was the craziest he'd ever heard, and he'd hired his gun for just about everything. His benefactor knew of Pole's deadly reputation, so a practical joke was out of the question, nor was the benefactor's sanity in doubt. Pole had to admit, he was curious what would happen, which was part of the reason he trudged through the cold.

Tula got going again. Silver Hollow appeared over the next hill. It was the usual assortment of rustic buildings he had seen from one end of the country to the other.

"Feel like a trot, Tula?"

He gently squeezed her sides with his heels. They closed the distance to Silver Hollow in under a minute. Pole slowed Tula back down to an easy walk as they entered the main street of the mining town. Lanterns strung across the store fronts bathed the main street in a yellow glow. Three covered wagons lined the street. Light spilled from the inn half-way down. Once there he tied Tula to the hitching post. The sign swinging over the entrance read: The Red Tree Inn. Pole went inside.

An assortment of bar patrons paused their card games, meals, and conversations to check out the tall stranger. He met their looks with a steely glare that was usually enough to discourage anyone from getting frosty. Pole Thompson's skill and speed with a gun was known throughout the west, but there was always someone who hadn't got the word.

The bartender greeted him with a forced smile. "Evening, stranger."

"Evening," Pole said. "Beer and supper, please."

The bartender looked put out as he called for the food to be readied, then poured a glass of beer. "I'm Virgil Matthews, proprietor."

"Pole Thompson."

If the name registered, Virgil didn't show it. "Passin' through kinda late, aren't you, Mr. Thompson?"

"I'm not passin' through, friend," Pole said. "Here for the night. Maybe more."

"I see," the bartender said. He gestured to a young man wiping tables. "Johnny, see to the man's horse, then tell Dina to get a room ready."

The boy nodded and ran out. Pole chuckled at his get-up-and-go.

"Youngsters always move fast for those pennies," Pole said.

"Good workers."

Pole heard that skittering sound he'd heard outside of town, this time along the ceiling and walls of the building. He looked around to see if anyone reacted to the sound. No one lifted their head or cocked an ear, so he dismissed it.

"Kind of busy tonight," Pole said. "Don't usually see so many people about at this hour, especially in this cold."

"Lots to do," Virgil said. "Snow season is coming upon us."

"It's been a while since I've been this far north," Pole said. "Towns like this more or less shut down for the winter, is that right?"

"More or less," Virgil said. "Which makes me curious."

"How so?"

"You said you're staying for one night, maybe more."

"Yeah?"

"If you've been up this way in the late fall, you know the snow can come for good at any time."

"I know."

"And once it's here for the winter, so are you."

Pole took a deep swallow of beer. "I know that, too."

"Mind if I ask your business here, Mr. Thompson?"

Thompson held Virgil with a stern look. Dina brought a plate of steak and potatoes. Pole grinned at her and began to eat.

"Sorry to be nosy," Virgil said.

Pole ate his meal, ignoring Virgil, who wiped the counter as he studied the big man. When the steak was halfway gone, Pole looked up.

"I'm chasin' legends, Mr. Matthews," he said, holding up his beer glass for a refill.

Virgil took the glass and refilled it. "Chasing legends here? Let me guess."

He set the beer down and leaned in close to Pole. His voice was low, comically secretive. "You're looking for a giant spider."

Pole froze in mid-chew, then slowly finished his bite of steak and swallowed.

"To be honest, Mr. Matthews, I didn't expect such a quick and level answer."

Another sound from outside. This time a sharp *thunk*. Again, no one reacted.

Virgil chuckled. "You're not the first, Mr. Thompson. We get a lot of visitors seeking the giant spider of Silver Hollow. We make a lot of money from the tourism. But, like you, they'll leave disappointed and never return."

"I see."

"So don't take this as rudeness, but your best bet is to eat up and head back south where it's warm. Leave us to our folklore."

"No offense taken," Pole said. "But I've come all this way, why don't you tell me where the legend came from?"

"Come now, Mr. Thompson. You're wasting your time. You want to get back to your family, don't you?"

"Don't have one. So as you can see, I have some time to kill."

Virgil Matthews studied Pole as he continued with his dinner. Pole looked up at him. Each man did his best to read the other's thoughts. Virgil nodded and smacked the bar as if he'd made a decision.

"Very well," Virgil said.

He looked over Pole's shoulder and spoke to two men who had been watching the conversation.

"Pat! Gordon!"

The two cowboys rose from their table and came to the bar, standing on either side of Pole.

"This here is Pole Thompson, fellas," Virgil said.

Pole sensed from their body language that they recognized his name. Good. Little chance of nonsense from them in that case. He finished the last of his vegetables and wiped his mouth.

"He wants to see the *spider*."

The men laughed, as did others in the room when they heard. Pole looked around. The laughter stopped.

"You see, Mr. Thompson. There was a spider, and it was a big one," Virgil explained. "But it was just a freak of nature. Killed some years ago. Some old cowboy killed it and stuck it to a fence post near the Holleck silver mine."

"How big?" Pole asked.

"About the size of your plate," Virgil said. "It was a nasty one, to be sure. Killed a couple of horses and a dog before it got done in by a rail-road spike. Word spread about the spider, and the size of it grew as the tale was told and retold. Sorry that's all we've got for you."

Pole studied the men's faces for any sign of deception.

"You don't believe me," Virgil said. "So be it. It's a cold night, but I'm sure you don't want your time wasted. Pat and Gordon here will take you on out to see it right now if you want."

Pole stood and put on his hat. "Very well. If it's all a tall tale like you say, I'll head south. If I'm not back in an hour, cancel the room, if you please."

"As you wish, sir."

Pole rode with Pat and Gordon south out of Silver Hollow. On their way Pole noticed several townspeople and tourists—he didn't know the difference—moving about on the boardwalks. Some seemed happy. Some miserable. Just a lot of people for a small town, Pole thought.

The road was rocky and uneven with many abrupt twists and turns. Pole rode side-by-side with Gordon as Pat led the way.

"Say, what was all that fidgeting noise on the walls and such?" Pole asked.

"I don't know what you mean," Gordon said.

Pole didn't press the issue. The rest of the ride continued in silence. The dusty road led downward into an old abandoned mining camp. Gordon rode ahead. Together he and Pat galloped to a crumbling mining hut and stopped. Pole kept Tula at a slow walk in the buffeting wind, taking in his surroundings, alert and wary. Mining supplies lay about, abandoned. Sifting plates, boxes of dynamite, troughs.

Tula was restless, but her trust in Pole was total. To his right he saw the opening to the silver mineshaft. In the darkness, it looked as if it led to the abyss. Tula trotted past the shaft. Pole joined Pat and Gordon by the old mining hut.

There Pole saw the shriveled carcass of a spider larger than any taran-tula he'd ever seen. It was dinner-plate sized all right, and dead as Moses. It was nailed to a support post. Pat and Gordon snickered. Pole looked at them and joined the laughter.

"I guess I've been taken for a ride, fellas," he said. "Tell Mr. Matthews I won't be needin' that room."

"Sure thing," Pat said.

Neither rider moved to leave. They watched Pole. Unease filled his gut. He subtly freed his gun hand from the reigns. Pat and Gordon were across from the mine shaft. Pole was in-between. Gordon lifted his chin and make a wet clicking sound with his tongue against his teeth. Pole frowned, confused.

The skittering sound came from the mine shaft, louder and faster than before. A giant spider, large as a horse, burst from the shaft.

"Lord almighty!" Pole said.

It crawled from the shaft on glistening black legs, moving at a terrifying speed. Pat and Gordon didn't move, only stared. Tula tapped about nervously, but didn't buck or rear back.

The spider raised its front legs and bared its dripping fangs in a savage display of menace. Pat and Gordon grinned, eager to see the spider devour the cowboy.

With only a seconds gone by from the spider's appearance, Pole drew his pistol and fired, hitting the spider in its open mouth. The creature roared and shrunk back. The two cowboys watched, mouths agape.

Pole watched the wounded monster dart around, confused and furious, trying to escape, trying to attack, its primal senses desperate for some survival option. Two more shots from Pole's pistol and the monster was dead in a cloud of dust.

Pat and Gordon froze in shock as Pole shifted his pistol to them.

"Stay still, boys," he told them. "You ain't fast enough. Even though you got me outnumbered."

Slowly, he led Tula close to the mineshaft entrance. He listened, drawing his other gun and aiming it at the darkness. All he heard was the wind.

"How many more?" he asked.

They were silent.

Pole shot Gordon in the arm. He fell from his horse with a scream.

Pole aimed at Pat, who held up his hands in defense.

"Stop! All right! There's at least a dozen!"

"A dozen?" Pole moved away from the entrance. "Why'd you bring me out here? Why the trap?"

"We don't call the shots, mister."

"What're the other critters waiting for? Why don't they all come out at us?"

"It ain't time."

Gordon staggered to his feet. Blood oozed from between his fingers as he clenched his wound.

"Ain't time, huh?" Pole said. "Fine. Let's get back to town. Move it!"

Pole replaced his spent cartridges. "And don't try to run ahead. You'll never make it."

The somber men led the way back to Silver Hollow. Pole watched their slouching shoulders. No doubt their job was to feed him to the spider. They had failed. The other spiders stayed in the shaft because it wasn't time for them to come out. What reason would that be? Virgil Matthews could be sure Pole Thompson would ask and expect an answer. If the two men in front of him wanted him dead, the town wanted him dead.

He thought about getting out. Being outnumbered by a pair of flatfoots was one thing, being outnumbered by an entire town was not a smart risk.

But he had the spider. No matter how crazy things had gotten. The huge money he had been offered was for one of those legendary giant spiders, dead or alive. A lifetime of riches lay on its back by the mineshaft, its long legs folded in. If he survived the night, he would take it to San Francisco with him.

The townspeople watched in shock as Pole returned alive. Back at the Red Tree Inn, Pole escorted Pat and Gordon into the saloon. Virgil was speechless.

"Surprised to see me, Virgil?" Pole said with a smile.

"I am indeed," Virgil said, glaring at the two men.

Pole ordered Pat and Gordon to sit, then raised his pistol and emptied it at the bar. Bullets shattered the wide mirror, along with bottles of beer and whiskey. Patrons screamed as the pistol boomed and glass exploded and rained down on the floor. Pole drew his other pistol.

"Everyone stay where you are," Pole said when he had everyone petrified.

"Now, Virgil," he said as he stalked the bartender with long, heavy footsteps. The bartender backed up against the wall. "I don't like bein' lied to. I don't like bein' tricked. And I sure as hell don't like being led into a nest of spiders the size of beef cattle!"

"You killed one?" Virgil asked.

"They ain't bulletproof!"

Virgil raised his palms in supplication. "Mr. Thompson, you must understand."

"Why didn't the other spiders come after me?"

"Because they come to us when they're ready," Virgil said. "They jumped you there because it's forbidden territory."

Pole looked around the saloon. "Everyone sit down. If I don't see both of your hands on the table, I'll shoot you."

Everyone quickly obeyed. Pole tipped his hat back and sat at the bar. "Virgil, in my line of work, I see people at their most vulnerable and their most honest. I can tell when a man is tellin' me the truth or when he's just tellin' me what I want to hear. I know this from years of seein' the last look on people's faces, you hear me?"

Virgil nodded vigorously.

"Am I to take it the spiders are gonna do something tonight?"

"Yes."

"So our time is short?"

"It is."

"Then you better tell me the story fast." He cocked his pistol "Don't lie."

Virgil wiped his hands on his vest, at first trying to think of a way out. Pole's gun hand was steady and his eyes didn't blink. There was no choice.

"Silver miners found 'em. Five generations ago," Virgil said. "The miners broke through a tunnel and out they came. Only one man made it out. Spiders killed most of the men of Silver Hollow. Our ancestors, they thought they were dead for sure. But those things, they have a way of talkin' to humans. Like through our minds."

Virgil waited to see how all of this was received. Pole didn't move. Still didn't blink.

"Anyway," Virgil went on. "It was through this mind-talk, as we call it, that the spiders told them all they wanted was their blood."

"That's all?" Pole asked.

"Sounds funny put that way, I know. But they only needed enough for their hibernation. They didn't care who they took it from. Our forefathers could give it, or they could find someone else to give it."

"How much does a person need to give?"

"All of it," Virgil said. "It was talked about, and when a group of hunters on their way to Canada came through, they were fed to the spiders. The townspeople were left alone. That's how they worked it from then after. That's how we work it still."

"Lord almighty," Pole said. "Is that why I see so many sour-faced travelers here?"

Virgil nodded. "They were taken from wagon trains and such. Brought here to feed the spiders. The spiders don't take everyone, just what they need. Anyone the spiders don't take are free to go."

"Because who would believe 'em?"

"That's right. I suppose that's how the legend spread," Virgil said. "Some famous people never made it out of Silver Hollow. Brian O'Brien, remember him?"

"Card shark and gunfighter. Disappeared."

Virgil nodded with a grim smile.

"Met his end here, I take it," Pole said.

"Along with Lady Diamond and her gang. Comanche raiding parties. Lots of stories ended here. The spiders protect us in exchange for the blood we give them."

"So where are these things from?"

"They ain't from here."

"I figured that. So where? Africa? Mexico?"

"I mean they ain't from *here*. Planet Earth."

"Likely as not they're from the abyss," Pole said. "Why not kill 'em? I saw boxes of dynamite stacked right by the old mining hut."

"Because there's more to the story, Mr. Thompson. You see, their venom kills when put right into the blood. But if you drink it—"

"I don't believe it."

"—it enters the blood in a more refined way, with amazing results."

Now Pole felt fear. "How amazing?"

Virgil smiled. "Mr. Thompson, *we* are the generation that first met the spiders."

Pole stood to his feet, feeling the momentum shift away from him and to his hosts. "That can't be. You said five generations! That's gotta be over one hundred years ago!"

"More like a hundred and fifty."

Pole stared at him, speechless.

"The spider venom not only keeps us alive, it keeps us from aging," Virgil said.

Pole shook his head in disgust. "One hundred and fifty years of sending innocent people to those things."

"Are you implying we face God's judgment, Mr. Thompson? You think we didn't pray and rend our garments for divine relief? None came. He abandoned us. We made an accord with beings who keep their word."

"That's horse puck, Virgil. That ain't how God works. Even a hellbound heathen like me knows that."

"Look behind you, Mr. Thompson."

Keeping his gun on Virgil, Pole turned to see a group of twenty-five people filing past the saloon, their faces fearful and miserable. Men, women, and children. Making sure everyone was still and behaved, Pole went out into the cold to see the frightened people being herded through the streets, like cattle. Locals with rifles and pistols made sure the group moved forward.

"If you fire on any of us, Mr. Thompson. We will gun down the innocent along with you. I'm sure we'll still have enough for the spiders," Virgil said. "You're coming with us. Don't worry. Chances are good they won't choose you. I'll bet the spiders fear you. Usually they instill such terror the victim freezes before they can react. By the time they know what's happening, the venom is entering their veins as their blood is leaving it."

The victims looked at Pole with longing, somehow sensing he was in a position to help.

"If you survive, you can go. That's how we've always done it."

Pole knew if he survived, he would kill every mother's son of them.

Either way, his final stand would not happen here, so he joined the wandering crowd. Their destination was the mining camp, Pole guessed. There the nest of spiders would come out to claim their hibernation feast. He shuddered to think what a ghoulish sight that would be.

As they walked out of town, Pole noticed a young woman draw up next to him. She held hands with a young girl. Pole gave her a grim smile.

"I'm Lucy."

"Ma'am."

Lucy pointed to the girl. "This is Mattie."

"Hello, Mattie."

"Can you save us?" Lucy asked.

"I don't know. Doesn't look good."

"They already took my husband."

Pole shook his head in disgust. "I'm sorry, miss."

"We thought they were bandits when they attacked our wagon train," Lucy said. "They just brought us here. We didn't know why. Then they took us out to the mining camp and gave my husband to the spiders. I guess it was to scare the rest of us into behaving until it was time."

She looked at him. The tears in her eyes made him vow revenge.

"You think they'll get us all?" she asked.

"I don't know," Pole said. "But I'll make a fight of it either way."

He carefully reloaded his pistols and holstered them. Two loaded guns, ready for battle. The last battle, if need be.

The group entered the remains of the mining camp. People started to cry and scream. Virgil and the others made that odd clicking sound, and the mineshaft rumbled for agonizing seconds before ebony spiders burst from the shaft, darting around as the people screamed.

Virgil raised his hand. The crowd quieted to whimpers and sniffles. The spiders assembled across from the people, baring their dripping fangs. Some people fainted. They would be taken for sure.

"I'm sorry for this, my friends, but it is necessary. If you survive, if the spiders pass you over, you are free to go."

Mattie clutched her mother. Lucy looked up to Pole, who had both pistols in hand. He rushed forward, breaking free from the front of the crowd. Lucy and Mattie followed.

With practiced steeliness and precision, he opened fire. He didn't miss once as the bullets tore into the creatures, blasting their heads off, shearing legs.

People screamed and ran away from the camp. The townsfolk opened fire, trying to hit Pole, but mostly hitting dirt along with some of their kidnapped victims. Pole sent some of his shots through the local gunmen, and the others ran and hid.

"Stay behind me!" he said to Lucy and Mattie.

The largest spider lunged at Pole. He fired three rounds into its head and it fell to the dirt. That drove the surviving spiders into a frenzy of blind terror. They fought and tore at each other to get back to the safety of the mineshaft. Pole aimed his shots to chase them down until the surviving creatures were back in the mine.

The chaotic battle was over. The cold night was silent save for the screams and moans of the wounded. Pole ordered the townsfolk to gather by the mining hut. He told the intended victims to gather the rifles and pistols. Soon the roles had reversed. Virgil, along with his ancient fellows, were now the prisoners.

Pole carefully removed a bundle of dynamite from the case.

"No!" Virgil shouted.

Pole lit a match. The fuse hissed to life with a blinding spark. He dropped the bundle into the mineshaft. Virgil and the others gaped in despair as the deafening explosion atomized any living thing below and caved in the shaft.

Virgil and the townsfolk stared dejectedly at the ground.

"We'll die," he said. "We'll grow old and die."

"You'll die all right," Pole said. "But you won't grow old."

Everyone huddled together as the wind picked up, bringing fat snowflakes with it. Pole looked at the sky. The bright glow of the moon rested behind a thick curtain of clouds.

"Gonna be a cold night. Coldest of the year so far, I'll reckon."

The snow came heavier. A thin white carpet graced the dirt.

"Since you folks are privy to making up rules on God's behalf, I'll do one for you," Pole said. "South from here, about ten miles, is the old Burnam pine tree. I'm sure you know the ol' landmark. Hell, maybe you planted it all those years ago."

Virgil was quiet.

"Anyway, you folks get down to that tree. Each one of you fetch me a pine cone and bring it back by morning."

"That's crazy. With this cold and snow, we'll freeze to death."

"That's another thing. Take off your clothes."

They looked dumbly at each other. Pole cocked his pistols.

"Take 'em off or I'll gut shoot each one of ya. Not a good way to go."

They stripped down their undergarments. Most of them were already violently shivering.

"Now go," Pole said. "If any of you make it back with my pine cones, well, we'll just figure that's a sign from God that we're supposed to forgive you."

All of them shivered.

"Now get!"

The defeated residents of Silver Hollow staggered off south toward Burnam pine. In minutes the night and swirling snow swallowed them.

Back in town, the survivors found warm places to sleep. Lucy asked Pole to stay with her and Mattie. He slept on the floor of a room in the

Red Tree Inn while they shared the bed.

Pole came down to the saloon the next morning. No villagers had returned. No pine cones were found. Lucy and Mattie joined him.

"None of them made it back?" Lucy asked.

Pole shook his head. "Nope."

"You sent them to their deaths, then?"

"I did."

". . . Good."

He looked at her surprised.

"I guess our wagon train will get going again," she said. "Although I don't know what Mattie and I will do. Miles always took care of us."

Pole was silent. Lucy smiled awkwardly. She kissed him on the cheek.

"Anyway," she said. "May the Lord bless you on your way."

She took Mattie by the hand. They left the inn. Pole watched them, then followed.

"Lucy?"

They turned back to him. He joined them.

"I'm taking one of those carcasses to San Francisco," he said. "Believe it or not, I have someone who's gonna pay me top dollar for it. And I mean top dollar."

"That's good for you."

"I could use some company for the trip."

She smiled.

"I'd be happy to pay you a good share," he said. "That would be enough to take care of you and Mattie for the rest of your lives."

"All right, then. Thank you kindly."

Pole Thompson appropriated a pair of covered wagons that would never again be used by the lost citizens of Silver Hollow. He bundled Lucy and Mattie on the first. He hitched the second wagon behind it. On that one he wrestled the carcass of the largest of the dead spiders. He covered it in curtains and blankets. It was too horrible for even him to look at.

The spider made Pole Thompson a rich man. His years of wandering and traveling ended with a grand house in San Francisco, built to his specifications. He retired his guns. He looked after Lucy and Mattie. When a respectable time of mourning had passed, Pole took Lucy as his wife and raised Mattie as his daughter.

With the jar of venom Pole had milked from the dead spider, the three of them spent several lifetimes of happiness together.

Bear Head Tower

Forest Ranger Hallie Dorsey strolled around the observation deck of Lookout Tower Four. Bear Head Tower, as it was more commonly known. Killian National Forest was one of the most dense, isolated forests in the country. Here, ten stories up in the cozy, cabin-like lookout, Hallie enjoyed isolation within isolation. Just as she liked it.

She sipped her evening coffee as a late summer gust of wind brushed her face. It was early September with a dusk temperature in the mid-sixties. The sun hung low, soon to dip below the Pacific Ocean, which was visible in the western horizon. It had rained non-stop the day before. The odds of spotting a forest fire were low, but she did a visual check anyway. As she expected, no smoke.

She had finished a long, uneventful day patrolling the back roads. No poachers. No lost hikers. No Bigfoot hunters in over their heads. The extreme isolation of the park attracted hardcore campers, hikers, and hunters. Serious sportsmen who respected nature and the rules. She also encountered those searching for some out-of-the-way hanky-panky. The only life she encountered that day was a mountain lion and a black bear. Not unusual for her, but always a thrill.

Despite her fatigue, she climbed the ten flights of tower stairs at the end of her shift to have a prime spot to watch the sunset beyond a sea of trees. Just her and God. And coffee.

A flicker of light flashed in her periphery. She looked away from the sunset in the direction the light originated. Nothing. She was about to turn back to the sun when it flashed again.

It was an orb of light. First silver, then red, then blue, then back to silver again. It continued to cycle through those colors. Hard to judge its size from a distance, which she guessed to be five or six miles. At first she thought it was a drone, some enterprising camper using it to get cool nature shots. Then a second orb arrived, flashing color like the first one. When a third orb joined the others, she walked around to the section of the deck facing the odd phenomenon.

The orbs darted around in a tight formation over the Keel Wilderness Area, named for Keel Hill in its center. Keel was the most dense part of the forest. Too dense for vehicles or horses. It was accessible only by foot, and camping was strictly at your own risk.

They couldn't be remote-controlled drones. They whizzed around each other at impossible speeds and angles. Random movements that in seconds coalesced into a unified, swirling pattern. The trio of orbs plummeted into the towering trees of Keel Hill and vanished.

Hallie frowned as she gulped the last of her coffee, staring at the spot where the orbs did their little show. She waited and watched for ten minutes. They did not reappear.

She went inside the tower and aimed the fire finder at the location while it was fresh in her mind. The fire finder was a tabletop device consisting of a glass-covered map of the park rounded by a rotating metal ring with opposing sights. Lining up a location through both sights would help you pinpoint a location on the map.

Usually, the device pinpointed smoke from a forest fire so crews knew where to respond. Hallie had used it to spot a UFO, which made her pause with the radio transmitter in her hand. What, exactly, was she going to tell dispatch when she called this in? Flying colored orbs without a park sticker? E.T. needs a phone? Not only would she risk trouble by wasting expensive park resources, her colleagues would lump her in with the Bigfoot loonies. That would be much worse.

Ridicule or no, she had a job to do. The anomaly should be checked out. Hallie put on her duty belt, which held her trusty Sig P229 pistol, and grabbed her backpack on her way out the door. She descended the endless flights of steps with a renewed sense of energy.

There was a mystery. While mystery always meant danger, it also meant the possibility of discovery. Either way, it was something new. And even if it came to nothing, it was an opportunity to get out into the woods, out into Keel Hill Wilderness, where the woods are lovely, dark and deep.

She reached the ground, breathing hard, and jogged to the Jeep. She drove the winding path toward Keel Hill, through tunnels of fir trees, and did the math. The fire finder placed the anomaly forty degrees west of north, seven miles away. It wouldn't be a long drive. There were trailheads leading into the Keel Hill area, but they were difficult to find unless someone showed them to you. The area was for experienced hikers. She was nervous about diving into such an isolated place at dusk, but figured she would be in and out soon enough.

Hallie stopped at a trailhead that was barely visible, even when parked right next to it. Just a hint of a clearing and a narrow path. She shouldered her backpack that included a first aid kit, back-up flashlight, and batteries. She moved swiftly through the familiar path. It was darker under the dense canopy of trees. She second-guessed her decision to investigate right away. It must be nerves. She was in good enough shape to hike the loop in about thirty minutes and be out, although her thighs would let her hear about it in the morning.

She stopped walking and looked around. The forest had gone silent. No birds or bugs singing out. Even the wind had stilled. All was quiet. She drew her weapon and held it ready, not so much for aliens, but for more terrestrial threats.

The base of Keel Hill was the loop-around point for the trail. She was almost there when a strobe of light made her jump. It flashed, then remained steadily lit. She glanced to her left. A basketball-sized orb floating just beyond a thicket of trees, only ten feet away. It cycled through silver, red, and blue. She squinted against the glare. It was beautiful, but it had an ominous presence. Hallie raised her pistol to it with shaking hands. What was the play here? Fire at an orb of light?

The other two orbs appeared, flickering with such speed that Hallie felt dizzy. The lights were brilliant and overpowering in the encroaching night. They circled her, floating at head level, accompanied by an intense humming that made Hallie's bladder weak. Pure terror gripped her mind. The temptation to fire in panic was strong.

She was near hyperventilation when the orbs finally eased away, further up the trail toward the hill. She put her hands on her knees and caught her breath. Her mind processed the feelings she'd had during the encounter. There was no mistake: the vibrations she felt from those things were pure evil. If this had happened in the lookout tower, she would have stayed put.

So now what? She was only a minute or two from Keel Hill. She had found the orbs. What was their intent? Were they leading her on? Warning her off? What could they do to her? Harm or kill? Would the Sig do any good against something that could maneuver like they did?

Her heartbeat returned to normal and her rational brain regained control. Her job was to watch over the forest. She would check out the hill, then go back and file a report. A carefully worded report to avoid any impressions of the supernatural. But something was off here. It should be mentioned in case park patrons were in danger.

Keel Hill was unique in that its shape was unusually angular and symmetrical. Hard to tell under the thick foliage, but if you looked close enough and took the time to walk around it, you could see it. Some Bigfoot hunter types theorized it was a lost pyramid, overgrown by the centuries with grass, moss, and trees. Hallie could only chuckle at what the geologists must think of that.

She stood at the base of the hill and looked around. Darkness had almost claimed the forest in full, but there was enough remaining light to examine the area. No orbs. No evil presence. Maybe it was disorientation. Nothing seemed out of the ordinary, except for a felled tree on the slope. The tree was sturdy. No way to tell what had pulled it up. She moved in to check it out.

The uprooted tree had come up roots and all and looked recently torn out. It left a jagged opening in the slope. Hallie stood before the gaping hole. Her flashlight revealed a large, deep cavity. She squatted and looked in. It burrowed down for a few feet, then angled horizontally into the hill. The flashlight beam disappeared into its depths.

"A cave?" she asked herself.

She wished she had backup. It was a bad idea to enter the tunnel (or cave, or whatever) alone, but she knew that's what she would do.

Aiming her weapon and flashlight forward, she shimmied down the hole and maneuvered until she was in the horizontal section. It was high enough for her to stand upright. She shook her head in wonder, curious how the park administration would deal with this discovery.

Her boots crunched along the floor of the tunnel as she moved forward. She looked back every few steps as she rethought the wisdom of entering so deep into the hill. Her footfalls took on a hollow, metallic thump. She froze. She tapped the floor with her toe. No question about it—she wasn't on soil anymore, but a metal pathway. She swept the flashlight around the walls of the cave, which only confirmed what the sounds of the floor told her. The walls were made of smooth, metal sheeting. She was in an artificial corridor under Keel Hill.

Decision time. Run back? Or move forward? She took stock of her emotions. Her heart raced and her breathing rushed along. The urge to know, to discover, was too strong. She continued along the corridor.

The flashlight illuminated a portico up ahead. It opened to a crossing hallway. She stepped through the corridor into the hallway and looked left and right. The hall stretched into darkness either way. By her best guess, she was close to the heart of Keel Hill. She was left-handed. That was as good a reason as any to make a left turn.

Her confidence grew as she went along. She quickened her pace. There were no warning signs that this was a forbidden government installation. Had she seen that, she would have turned around and forgot she was there. Not only were there no warning signs from Uncle Sam, there were no signs at all.

The hall led her to a spacious opening. She gasped.

She was on the bridge of a ship. There were display screens, controls. Buttons and levers. Chairs. Piping snaking along the ceiling. All of it dark and silent. The chairs, she noticed with unease, were much to tall and thin for an average human. Who, or what, sat in chairs like that?

A new light source flickered around the room. The three orbs were back, along with the ominous, evil sensation that came with them. They floated into the room, moving with greater deliberation than before. Hallie raised her gun, hoping it would be useful for defense, should it come to that.

The orbs eased out of the bridge and down the hall that brought Hallie in. She examined the dark, empty bridge. The shifting light glowed from the hallway. They were waiting for her. Seeing no other way out, she followed.

They led her out of the bridge and into another room. She entered and banged her thigh against a structure of some kind. She cursed and hissed and shined her flashlight.

The yellow light caught two long, skinny red legs lying on an open capsule bed. She held her breath as she moved the beam up the body. It looked like a humanoid stick bug with red skin. The face was demonic and bat-like. The eyes were closed. It looked asleep.

The orbs rotated in a circle over the thing's head. The vibrations intensified. Hallie couldn't run. Her legs were locked in fear. The thing's eyelids fluttered and opened to reveal obsidian eyes that glanced around the room, confused.

A row of tiny bulbs lit up along the ceiling, revealing long rows of capsules on Hallie's left and right, all of them full of these grotesque beings.

She couldn't see the far end of the corridor, although Keel Hill was only so big. There had to be hundreds of these things laid out in neat rows. Through her terror, she came to what seemed to be the only conclusion—she was on a ship of hibernating aliens, sleeping long enough for the forest to claim their ship long before the first humans explored it.

Hallie's gaze returned to the original being, which now looked directly at her. It's expression, best she could tell, was one of curious hatred.

"Hi," Hallie said, feeling foolish.

The creature stirred in its capsule at the sound of her voice. The orbs moved along the other capsules, rotating as they had with this one. Activating them. Other beings shifted and stretched.

Hallie decided it was time to leave. She jogged away without a good-bye. The ship wasn't a maze of corridors. It was a basic down-the-hall-and-to-the-left path to escape. Despite her head start, she heard several pairs of footfalls on the metal walkway close behind. They were in pursuit.

She made it to the end of the exit corridor and into the cave, relieved at the feel of soil under her boots again. She panicked as her hips got stuck trying to crawl out of the hole leading up to the forest night. She wriggled free as the thumping footsteps bore down on her.

Darkness cloaked the forest as she pulled herself out and rolled down the slope of the hill. She jumped to her feet, aiming her weapon at the hole as she backed away. She still had her flashlight, and thought she knew the path well enough to run for it in the dark.

She ran a short distance and slid to a stop when she saw two of the spindly red beings blocking her retreat. Compared to her height, she estimated they were seven feet tall. Crunching leaves and breaking twigs sounded behind her. The creatures poured out of the hole behind her, cutting her off.

She raised the pistol.

"Can you understand me?" she asked. "Do you know what this is?"

She didn't have enough ammo to kill them all, but one blast should be enough to frighten them.

"Move, or I'll shoot."

She gestured with her hands for them to move aside. They did not. More creatures gathered behind her. They closed in. Feeling threatened, she aimed her pistol at the sky and fired. The report deafening her ears in the still woods. The creatures showed fear at the blast and flash, just as she'd hoped. She hoped to escape without killing visitors from another world.

"Can we talk?" she asked. "I'm thinking friendly thoughts. Can you tell?"

They didn't look at each other. They glared at her. Unknown beings or no, they gave off an insidious vibe, just like the orbs.

She ran off the path and into a cluster of trees. They chased her like hunting dogs. She briefly looked back and saw them struggling with the branches as they came after her. She grinned. They were in her territory, after all. She kept close to the hiking path, figuring the hard way would keep them back.

It looked like the plan was going to work when clawed fingers swiped at her back. They had caught her. She yelled in pain. Before they could finish her off, an enormous shape rampaged through the trees. This was new, another player in the game. The newcomer lifted her by the backpack and tucked her under a long, hairy arm. It carried her on huge strides like a newborn babe on through the forest. A stinging, skunk-like stench burned her nostrils. The aliens continued to chase.

Hallie and the thing carrying her broke into a clearing. It tossed her to the ground. She dropped the pistol and fell hard on her stomach. The wind rushed out of lungs. She struggled to get her air back as the creatures filed into the clearing. What the giant thing their overlord?

The chase was over. There was no escape. She hoped whatever they had in mind would be quick. A mass of leaves and branches hid her gun on the forest floor. Her breathing returned to normal. She found her flashlight. She aimed the beam around the clearing and lit up an enormous furry being standing at the edge. It responded to the light with a low rumbling moan.

"Oh my God."

How many times had she told excited hunters and campers that the hairy beast they saw was just a black bear? That the growling they heard was a mountain lion? The screaming just an eagle? The giant footprints the work of pranksters? That's what her colleagues would say if she survived the night and told them about it. But she knew what a black bear looked like. What an eagle or mountain lion sounded like. It was her job to know.

She had a lot of apologies to write.

The Bigfoot was taller than the alien creatures. Had to be nine feet tall. Too big to be a black bear. The giant beast took a lumbering step forward, a stride so long it could have stepped over her lengthwise. She backed away. A nervous ripple shot through the aliens.

Hallie giggled like a madwoman. The absurdity of the situation eclipsed her fear.

"You guys gonna fight over me? You sure know how to make a girl feel special. Why don't you fight for me, huh? See who wins."

And give me a chance to slip away.

The Bigfoot only needed one more step to loom over the mass of creatures. More heavy footsteps thudded through the trees. Branches snapped and whipped. Hallie swept her light around to reveal six more Bigfoot entering the clearing.

The Bigfoot and the aliens regarded each other for several uncomfortable seconds. The first Bigfoot let out a piercing scream. The creatures swarmed the Bigfoot and attacked.

Hallie covered her ears at the awful sound. She crawled away to avoid the ferocious fight. In the chaos, there was no way to know the right escape path, so Hallie withdrew to the edge of the clearing.

The creatures tittered like insects. The Bigfoot roared and screamed. Alien claws drew blood from the giants. The Bigfoot were far more powerful than the creatures and snapped their long limbs and torsos like twigs.

Hallie felt an odd dissonance in her brain, a sense that a thought pattern was being established. The creatures probably. No match for the Bigfoots' strength, they tried to awaken their mental powers. Having just awakened, they were not yet at full power. All of this was Hallie's guess.

Retreat would have been a better idea for the creatures. The Bigfoot defeated them. Soon alien bodies were piled in an insane stack of red, broken bodies. The Bigfoot caught their breath and settled down. They worked together to carry the bodies away. Hallie smiled to herself, knowing at that moment she could never prove what had happened. The Bigfoot would make sure the entrance to the alien ship—which was confirmed to be the underground pyramid the loonies suspected—was closed up and invisible, the bodies done away with.

When the bodies were carried away, only the original Bigfoot remained. Hallie gingerly raised the light to its neck, being careful to keep from shining it directly into the giant's eyes. It watched her for a few seconds, as if trying to decide what to do with her. It was the first real sense of danger Hallie had since the Bigfoot came from the trees. However, the thing turned to leave without ceremony.

"Thanks," Hallie said, wondering if it was foolish to speak.

The Bigfoot turned and looked at her again. She tried to decode an expression in the giant's face, but it turned again and disappeared into the woods.

The exertion and intense emotional ordeal had sapped her energy. She drove back to Bear Head Tower. It took all she had left to make up the ten stories' worth of steps.

Her uniform reeked of Bigfoot odor. She shimmied out of her clothes and set them on an open window ledge to air out. The smell was her only evidence of the encounter. She didn't care. No way would she tell anyone. If she had witnessed an attempted and repelled invasion of Earth, that would be between her, the creatures of the forest, and the creatures of some other planet.

Again she walked out onto the observation deck, this time with vodka from a forbidden flask instead of coffee. The liquor soothed her nerves as the evening breeze chilled the sweat on her arms and legs. The stars reigned overhead, a thick carpet of glitter free from the concealment of city lights.

She stood watching the Keel Hill Wilderness Area. In the moonlight she saw the prominent hill. Trees jostled around its base. Must be the wind. She gasped when the three orbs shot up from the hill, one after the other in a beeline for the heavens. She watched as they grew smaller and smaller. Soon they blended into the silver glow of the moon.

Hallie marveled how that bright, full moon used to seem so far away. After tonight, it seemed much closer. She wondered what else lurked among the uncountable stars that surrounded it.

The Demon of Hallowtide

Through the forest, past farm fields and pastures, overlooking the village of Audemar, standing high and majestic on a headland jutting into the sea, rose the towering castle of Lord Robert Howe, Marquess of Ormond.

It was the Eve of All Hallows, the first day of Hallowtide, a three-day festival of remembrance for the dead. The holiday also marked the bringing in of the harvest, the end to the warmth of spring and summer, and the start of winter darkness.

On this night the barrier between the spirit world and the world of flesh and stone was blurred, almost non-existent. For one night, spirits of the departed returned to the earthly soil they once walked. Some longed only to see their loved ones again. Some were lost and confused. Some returned for trickery and evil, for further indulgence in dark deeds they committed in life.

In the small church on the outskirts of of Audemar, Father Aldun led a series of prayers for the dead. Candles were lit in the church and among the gravestones. Bonfires lined the dirt roads of the village so wandering souls would not get lost on their nightly sojourn. Costumes worn by the living made them unrecognizable to the dead. Tradition held that even the spirits themselves could don a costume, and one never knew when the spirits walked among them on All Hallow's Eve.

Harvest that year was even more bountiful than the last. The return of the knights and soldiers from the last victorious war accompanied the previous rich harvest. Last year had been one of peace, the first any living person had experienced. It was a time of great celebration, bounty, and joy. While the spirit of gratitude and celebration was genuine, there was no question the exuberant rituals served to keep the dark spirits of the night at bay.

Lord Howe had the favor of his king and his people. He very much looked forward to the All Hallow's Eve party in his castle. Gifts from his subjects' yearly labors stocked the banquet—fruits, vegetables, fish, breads, and cakes. He had barrels of ale. There were enough entertainers to keep everyone laughing and dancing through the night. The plentiful harvest provided more than enough to indulge weekend festivities and store up for the long, cold winter.

He looked forward to seeing everyone in costume. It was a challenge to figure out who lurked behind what mask. He rarely guessed better than half.

A chilly wind came through the window from the sea. Lord Howe, in his costume of red and black robes, stepped out onto the balcony and looked out into darkness. He heard the waves crashing in the shadows. Darkness hid the moon that night, adding to the sinister aura of the event.

"Your mask, My Lord."

Robert returned to his room to find Juliana, Lady Howe—his wife—holding out his mask.

"I do think you're taking a risk dressing up as such a thing," she said. The mask was the angular, pointed visage of the devil himself.

"I am full of confidence, my dear. It has been a bountiful time for us, but it is time to expand, to reach higher."

"Are we not rich enough?" she asked with a wink.

"There are always more coins to caress. More lands to conquer."

"It sounds as though you have plans for us."

"The king is weak. He depends on me totally."

"Maybe it's best we talk about this when there aren't so many people in the castle."

"You're probably right, my dear," he said as he put on the mask.

"What will Father Aldun think?" she asked.

Lord Howe adjusted the mask. It covered his head.

"The priest is aware that tonight is a night of expression and release," he said. "A little transgression is in order. I will set the example."

The mask's hinged jaw moved up and down when he spoke.

"We all have our way of expressing transgression, I suppose," Juliana said.

She strapped on her own mask. Her raven hair spilled over and around the eerie, blank face. She stood barefoot in a simple black chemise.

"What do you think?" she asked, her voice muffled by the mask.

"I think you are more unsettling than I am."

She twirled around. The dress had a series of hidden vertical slits up to the chest which sailed out parallel to the floor as she spun, looking like spokes in a wheel, showing plenty of her white skin.

Lord Howe chuckled at his wife's daring. "You're in no position to ask me what the priest will make of *my* costume."

"Then keep him distracted should I decide to dance."

"Are you sure our people are worthy to gaze upon the flesh of a noblewoman?"

"No, but neither are you, kind sir. However, it is—as you call it—a 'night of transgression.'"

As Lord and Lady Howe shared their secrets, the four knights in their service stood watch on the castle walls. Sir Simon faced the sea. He had ordered the torches along the eastern wall extinguished so his eyes could adjust to the darkness. He turned in the direction of approaching footsteps. It was Sir Berold, the grizzled dean of the knights, who walked with a slight limp.

"The sea is empty, I presume?" Sir Berold asked.

Sir Simon nodded and returned his gaze to the hidden sea. Sir Berold wasn't surprised. Sir Simon's quiet nature was well-matched to his dark, severe features.

"In that case, let's collect our brothers," Sir Berold said. "Lord Howe says having us on patrol will make the villagers superstitious."

Sir Simon walked with Sir Berold without protest. They scanned the grounds outside, then watched the villagers scurry about within. At the corner of the castle wall they pivoted onto the northern wall where the hulking outline of Sir Hugh stood against the light of flickering fires from the courtyard below.

"Sir Hugh!" Sir Berold called out.

"I'm not leaving my post," Sir Hugh said, his voice as gruff as his face.

"Lord Howe's orders, my friend," Sir Berold said as he and Sir Simon joined him.

"The northern border is tense," Sir Hugh said. "Lord Howe knows this. A moonless night is the perfect cover for an invasion."

"On the Eve of All Hallows?" Sir Berold said in disbelief. "What army would start a war at the beginning of winter? Or march with the souls of the dead about?"

"A desperate one."

"You're jittery, Sir Hugh. Come along, let's enjoy the feast. The winters are long."

Sir Hugh scanned the horizon once more before grunting and grudgingly following his fellow knights. They walked the empty wall and angled down the western wall, the wall that faced down to the village, the fields, and the forest beyond.

"No soldiers on watch? None?" Sir Hugh asked.

"The celebration is for everyone," Sir Berold said, the irritation growing in his voice.

Sir Hugh sighed and kept further complaints to himself.

They joined the fourth and final knight, Sir Ralf, who looked down at the bonfires and costumed villagers crossing the drawbridge and entering the inner castle wall.

"Any foreign spies among them, Sir Ralf?" Sir Berold asked.

Sir Hugh frowned, knowing the question was a dig at him.

"All quiet, Sir," Sir Ralf said.

Sir Ralf had only two years ago been a squire. He was elevated to knighthood by Lord Howe and had won his brother knights' respect with his bravery in battle. He was anxious to please and eager to fight.

"Very well," Sir Berold said. "Let's join the festivities."

The four knights left the evening watch. They descended the stone steps to the inner grounds of the castle. Admiring looks from men, women, and children followed the tall knights in their reflecting armor. They encountered dancing, drinking, and shrieks of celebration among the bonfires. The knights collected tankards of ale that they drank on their way to the castle entrance.

Inside, Lord and Lady Howe came down to the great hall to much applause. Lady Howe made sure to lift her knees higher than necessary on her way down the stairs, showing her white thighs to the appreciative villagers, who whooped and cheered in beer-fueled appreciation.

Father Aldun rose his eyebrows at the sight of female skin and ungodly masks. No one took notice of him. Not tonight. He would endure the celebration for a few more minutes to offer his benediction, then leave. As his bishop had to constantly remind him, this was a night to let off some steam. It was best to let it happen in a controlled setting rather than have the proverbial steam escape at a more inopportune time.

The Howes stood behind the grand dining table on the elevated platform. Servants lined their table and the others with roast pig and sections of a giant deer Lord Howe had felled himself. The celebrants gathered around the other tables, admiring the meat along with the loaves of bread, the cooked fish, and plenty of cakes.

Lord Howe beckoned Father Aldun to offer the benediction. The priest stood on the platform as the musicians quieted and the chattering stopped. As soon as the prayer was over, a rumbling thunder shook the castle.

Sir Hugh and Sir Berold shared a look.

"Thunder?" Sir Hugh asked. "The skies are clear."

The villagers screamed as the thunder intensified, sounding like thousands of cannons firing at once. Purple lightning flashed through the windows. Lord Howe gathered Juliana in his arms as the roaring crescendoed to heavy splashing.

"The moat!" Sir Ralf said.

The knights ran from the hall, gesturing a team of soldiers to follow. Father Aldun joined them.

"Please be calm, my friends," Lord Howe said as panic rippled through the villagers. "Merely a crack of thunder or shaking of the earth. It's over now. No matter what, our brave knights are capable of defending against any threat."

He impatiently gestured for the music to resume, which it did. The villagers grumbled to each other. Lord Howe overheard talk of bad omens and God's judgment. Maybe the party should be canceled. The band played terribly with shaking hands. Lord Howe took Juliana by the hand.

"We are here to revel!" he shouted.

He shared a knowing look with Juliana. Lady Howe twirled faster than before. The shocked villagers laughed in disbelief, then cheered, and the momentary terror was forgotten.

The four knights and the priest ran across the drawbridge and along the banks of the moat. Ten soldiers followed, carrying torches to light the water.

"The splash came from the northwest," Sir Ralf said.

They ran along the moat until they reached the northwest corner of the castle wall.

"See there!" said Sir Hugh. "The water is disturbed. Look at the waves."

"Something big landed in the water," Sir Berold said.

"There!" Sir Simon said, speaking for the first time that night.

It bobbled in the water like a giant cork, only it was roughly spherical and glistened in the reflected firelight.

"What is it?" Father Aldun asked, making the sign of the cross.

"Must be six feet across," Sir Hugh said.

"A chunk of ice," Sir Ralf said.

"Impossible," Father Aldun said. "A piece of ice fallen from the sky? A curse, that would be."

A few curious villagers peered down from the castle walls.

"Go back," Sir Hugh said.

The villagers disappeared.

Sir Hugh turned to the soldiers. "Run down to the port, get the grappling hooks from the ships and one lifeboat."

While the soldiers ran out to their errand, the knights and the priest examined the ice ball from a distance.

"The ice is mostly clear," Sir Hugh said. "We can see that much."

"There's something frozen within it," Father Aldun said.

"Don't start rumors, Father," Sir Berold said. "You'll be held responsible if you start a panic."

"I'm only speaking of what I see with my own eyes," Father Aldun said.

"He's right," Sir Hugh said. "Some kind of animal is inside."

"But how?" Sir Ralf asked. "How was it frozen and how was it thrown into the air?"

"Some new weapon of the enemy?" Sir Hugh asked.

"Let's stop wondering until we can get it closer." Sir Berold said.

The soldiers returned with the grappling hooks and the lifeboat. The knights didn't hesitate to enter the boat and paddle out to the ice ball. In less than a minute they were next to it, the ice scraping against the boat's wooden hull. The knights examined the frozen object, holding their torches close.

"Indeed, there's something trapped within it," Sir Ralf said.

"Is it dangerous, you think?" Sir Simon asked.

"Does it matter?" Sir Hugh said. "Whatever it is, it's surely dead."

"We're assuming it was a living thing," Sir Berold said. "Could be a mass of tree branches for all we know. We have to get it into the light."

In the great hall, the party had grown rowdy again. Lord Howe smiled under his mask as he surveyed the dining, drinking, and dancing. He glanced at Juliana, her face obviously unreadable under her empty mask. Her body, however, was still.

"Are you all right, My Lady?" he asked.

"Bring it in," she said, her voice flat.

"Bring what in?"

The party stirred when Sir Berold returned. They continued to celebrate, but whispered among themselves as the knight walked straight to the head table. Sir Berold told of the discovery and his recommendation to bring the ice into the great hall where there was plenty of light to examine the object and melt it down.

Lord Howe looked slowly at Juliana, recalling her order to "bring it in." He looked back to Sir Berold.

"You're sure there's no danger?" he asked the knight. "What does the priest say?"

"The priest has dark speculations, My Lord."

"And you and the other knights?"

"Nothing can live in solid ice, assuming it contains a creature of some kind," he said. "But our swords will be ready, just in case."

Lord Howe looked at his wife again. The blank mask turned slowly to look at him.

"Bring it in, then," he said. "But under heavy guard."

"Of course, My Lord."

The knights, aided by the soldiers, used the grappling hooks to tow the ice ball to the edge of the moat and haul it up to dry land. They wrestled it onto a horse-drawn spit and dragged it through the courtyard, into the great hall.

By the light of torches and the great fireplace, the cloudy, icy sphere obviously contained some sort of humanoid figure, like a child or a small man. The villagers gasped in awe, looking to Lord Howe to see how to react, but his face, like theirs, remained hidden behind his mask. The Marquess and his wife, along with the knights and the priest, were wary, but calm, so the villagers remained calm as well.

Father Aldun sidled up next to the Marquess.

"My Lord, are the masks still appropriate?" he asked.

"We will not yield to fear, Father," Lord Howe said. He motioned to the soldiers. "Set it by the fireplace. We'll let it melt."

The soldiers did as ordered. Villagers gathered around it. The knights admonished them not to touch the ice. There was endless speculation as to what the thing could be. The ice was not clear enough for a definitive answer. Some thought it was a monster from the underworld, come to judge them all for their licentiousness. Some thought it merely a poor soul frozen from the north, and some kind of freak weather had brought it on the wind. Lord Howe had no idea and didn't want to risk foolishness by speculating. Again he saw his wife staring transfixed at the ice, and he considered having it hauled out.

Father Aldun stood praying silently over the ice, making the sign of the cross. When he looked up, Lord Howe beckoned him to the table.

"What would be the church's position on this?" he asked the priest.

Father Aldun looked the ice sphere and back to Lord Howe, his face betraying his cluelessness.

"An animal. A fallen angel," the priest said. "I don't know. If it is demonic, the Lord has given us power over it. If it is an unknown animal, the knights are more than able to slay it."

"And if it's God's judgment?"

"Then enjoy the revelry, My Lord. For this is our last night on Earth."

Lord Howe stood and looked out over the hall, seeing that everything had gone quiet. The people looked to him, waiting. Once again, he ordered the party to resume. Quietly, he instructed the knights and soldiers to stay close to the ice and for Father Aldun to also be near. He rotated Juliana's chair so she couldn't see the thing. Her body relaxed.

"I don't like the effect this thing has on you, My Lady."

"It fascinates me is all," she said. "Not to worry, My Lord."

Two of the villagers hit upon the idea of boiling water to pour on the ice to hasten its melting.

Sir Berold glanced at Lord Howe, who nodded his permission for them to proceed.

As the minutes passed, the object in the ice became less a source of fear and more one of fascination. They took bets on what was in the ice. Some speculated that it might make for good eating.

The knights and the priest kept a close watch on the thing, pacing back and forth, swords drawn.

Lord Howe studied his subdued wife. The blank mask hid her eyes in shadow, but he sensed they were wide with eager anticipation.

"Do you wish to dance, my dear?"

"He has come down with great wrath," she said.

"Who?"

"The others are coming. A new reign on Earth."

Lord Howe slid her ale tankard away. "No more for you, love."

She didn't protest the loss of her drink. Her change in demeanor unsettled him. He stood and walked to the knights.

"Set a watch on the castle walls, Sir Berold," Lord Howe said, thinking of his wife's comment about others coming.

"Yes, My Lord."

Sir Berold set a team of soldiers up to the castle walls.

For a quarter of an hour, things continued on as normally as they could. Villagers continued to pour boiling water on the ice. The knights stood guard. Father Aldun maintained a silent prayer vigil. Lord Howe grew increasingly concerned with his wife's somnolence. It was useless to obstruct her view of the ice. She would change position to see it, so he gave up and let her stare. It was understandable if the thing's arrival had spooked her. Seeing the sphere's contents would surely break the spell. Otherwise, the people of the village danced and sang, bobbed for apples, and played games.

A shriek rang out from the crowd, and people ran away from the ice sphere. Lady Howe shot to her feet, her body tense. Lord Howe reached for her arm, but she had already raced around the edge of the table. He ran behind her and they joined the knights as they examined the ice.

"What is it?" Lord Howe asked as panic swept the hall.

Sir Berold pointed at the ice with a grim expression. Lord Howe looked down.

A small, red-skinned humanoid hand—approximately the size of an adolescent child's—protruded limply from the ice. It had three fingers and a thumb. Long black talons tipped the fingers.

The villagers, well-soaked with ale and frenzy, screamed and ran amok, shouting about the devil and demons.

Sir Hugh roared for silence. The bellowing of the big man had the desired effect. Screams died down to whimpers. Sir Berold nudged at the hand with the flat of his sword. Another ripple of fear stirred the crowd when he moved the small fingers.

"We're leaving," said a villager.

Murmurs of agreement rose from the others. People gathered their things. The knights looked to Lord Howe, who shrugged his shoulders in defeat.

As the gathered villagers made their way to the castle exit, a pair of soldiers rushed in.

"My Lord! We've come from the wall!"

"What is it?" Sir Berold asked.

"There are people gathered outside, watching the walls, coming toward the drawbridge," the soldier said.

"An army? Are they armed?" Lord Howe asked.

"No. Just people. Shuffling around, staring."

"We'll have a look," Sir Berold said. "Sir Simon, stay with the ice."

The knights ran from the hall. Villagers continued to gather and leave. The party was over. Lord Howe sighed in disappointment. He looked around for Juliana. Perhaps together, in the privacy of their chambers, they could still have a pleasurable evening.

He found her by the fireplace, pouring boiling water onto the ice sphere. Further melting freed the creature's arm and shoulder.

Sir Berold led his fellow knights to the top of the western wall. Anxious soldiers waited for them.

"I hope you know what to do here," said one of them.

The knights frowned as they looked down at the straggling crowd of men, women, and children. Their eyes were glazed and black as marbles. They were naked. Their mutated, contorted bodies made it hard to discern men from women. They kept their eyes on the castle, up at the knights and soldiers, expectant.

"Not of the village, I take it," Sir Hugh said.

No one recognized any of the people below.

"Dare we speculate where they came from?" Sir Ralf asked.

Sir Berold studied the people in silence for a moment. "Let's go down and see what their intentions are."

The knights and soldiers came down from the wall to find the villagers on the approach, ready to leave. The people froze when they saw the strange newcomers gathered at the far end of the drawbridge.

"Who are they?" a villager asked. "*What* are they?"

"State your business!" Sir Berold called out.

One of the wandering strangers, a woman, opened her mouth and bared her teeth in an expression so savage the villagers and even the knights took a step back. She let out a guttural hiss, and the others joined her.

"Lower the gate!" Sir Berold said. "Raise the drawbridge!"

The soldiers rushed to carry out the order.

"We'll be trapped in here with that thing!" a villager cried.

"You'd prefer your chances out there with them?" Sir Ralf asked.

"Back into the hall!" Sir Berold ordered.

The knights and soldiers herded the people back into the great hall. When they saw Lady Howe by the fireplace, they went quiet.

The ice had gone to water, and the creature lay on the floor, inert. Lord Howe watched from the table. Father Aldun stood at his side.

The knights stepped forward. Sir Hugh stepped in front of Juliana.

"Please step back, My Lady. Let us deal with it," he said.

The little imp—red-skinned, winged, fanged, sexless, and grotesque—appeared to be dead.

Sir Hugh looked at Lord Howe. "I think it's dead, My Lord."

"Get it out of here," Lord Howe said.

"Take it out and burn it," Father Aldun said.

Lady Howe reacted hysterically to those orders. She shrieked her opposition, and the knights had no choice but to restrain her. Lord Howe and the priest rushed to her. The villagers wailed in helpless fear. Lord Howe stopped short when his wife spat a growling hiss at him. The knights looked at each other.

"Things are complicated, My Lord," Sir Berold said.

The knight told Lord Howe about the new arrivals beyond the wall and how they had to raise the drawbridge.

"Very well," said the Marquess. "We'll deal with it right here. Dismember this thing. Throw the pieces in the fire."

Lady Howe screamed anew and fought against Sir Simon's grasp.

"Sir Simon," Lord Howe said. "Take the lady up to our chambers. Restrain her to the bed."

Sir Ralf joined Sir Simon. The knights wrestled her up the stairs to the Howe's private chambers. She continued to scream even after they left the room, and her cries echoed through the castle.

Lord Howe, doing his best to ignore his wife's torment, gestured to Sir Hugh to get rid of the creature.

"Perhaps I should rid us of the forces of darkness first," Father Aldun said.

Lord Howe nodded. "Of course. Thank you, Father."

The villagers quieted as Father Aldun started a prayer against any evil that came with the creature. Lady Howe continued to scream. Everyone did their best to ignore her.

At the sound of Father Aldun's prayer, the creature stirred. People backed away, gasping. The knights readied their swords. Father Aldun briefly lost his breath, but seeing the effect his words had, he pushed on against his fear.

The little imp jumped to its feet. A bolt of fear shook the exhausted villagers. The imp moved forward aggressively, but stopped short at the sight of four sword points aimed at its head. It looked up at the knights, which appeared as giants to the little creature that came up to their thighs. Father Aldun prayers continued urgently. The imp covered its pointed ears.

"Stop!" it said.

Everyone stared in fear at the hissing sound of the imp's voice.

Father Aldun continued, his prayers getting louder, more confident.

The imp screeched in frustration and leapt high into the air. It landed near the villagers and swiped at the nearest man with its long talons. The claws gashed at the man's leg, and he collapsed in pain and terror.

Sir Hugh swung his blade at the creature, and it barely ducked away. The large knight pressed in, determined to kill the thing. The other knights joined the attack, backing the imp into a corner. The swords. The prayers. It was trapped with no escape. It looked around frantically and saw Lord Howe at the head table. It relaxed and looked at the Marquess with fascination and disbelief.

The knights looked at each other, unsure what to make of imp's reaction. Father Aldun concluded his prayer with an order for the satanic imp to depart immediately.

"I don't have to leave, Father," the imp said. "You are not united in your wish to banish me."

Sir Hugh swung again, The imp jumped away to the head table. The knights rushed to protect Lord Howe, but he gestured them to stay.

"She wants me here," the imp said.

Everyone realized Lady Howe had stopped screaming.

"You look like my lord and master," the imp said, referring to the Marquess's costume. "I have power, you know. I came down with power from my master. I can give it to anyone I want."

"Silence!" Father Aldun shouted.

"Let him talk, you filthy hypocrite!" Lady Howe shouted from her room.

"My Lord," Father Aldun said. "Do not converse with this demon. It is a liar and speaks on behalf of the Father of Lies!"

Lord Howe turned to the imp and cleared his throat. "I don't need your power. My lands are prosperous and at peace."

The imp grinned an awful grin. "Good."

Father Aldun stepped between the imp and the Marquess. "It is our allegiance to the risen Christ that prevents us from making any accord with you. Nothing else."

He shot an admonishing look at the Marquess.

The imp studied the priest.

"Are you really a man of God? Is there anything hidden?"

The imp reached out its taloned hand to the priest. "If so, then you are immune to any harm I might try to bring to you."

Father Aldun stood his ground, but his forehead beaded with sweat, his breathing chopped.

The imp jumped up and clutched the priest's neck. Father Aldun tried to cry out, but the talons dug in deep. The knights rushed forward.

"Why bother?" the imp asked. It turned to the priest. "What is it? Drunkenness? Fornication? You made yourself weak."

Father Aldun collapsed to the floor dead. The villagers wailed in despair. The imp turned to the knights.

"And you brave men," it taunted. "Who among you is worthy of challenging me?"

Sir Hugh swung his blade and severed the imp's arm. The creature looked at the stump wide-eyed in shock. The knights pressed in.

"Perfection is not required of us, demon," Sir Berold said. "I don't know what dwelt in the heart of Father Aldun, but you have overplayed your hand with us."

"Filthy thing," Sir Hugh said. "I will make a feast of you."

The imp turned to Lord Howe. "I offer you power. It will grow until the world is yours."

Plates of food appeared on the head table, then on the other tables. Roasted birds and pigs. Pies and cakes. Exotic foods from unknown lands that nonetheless looked delicious. Stacks and piles of treats.

"Shut up, demon!" Sir Hugh yelled. "My Lord, do not listen. The priest was right. He is a liar."

Gold coins rained down from an invisible source above. They pinged to the stone floor like metallic rain. The villagers raced to gather it up.

"It is cursed!" Sir Ralf said.

The oak barrels swelled with ale until the foaming liquid burst from the spigots and seams.

The villagers raced around the great hall, gathering coins and gorging on food and drink. The knights looked at each other, unsure what to do. They looked at Lord Howe, who smiled at the happiness of the people.

Sir Berold ran to Lord Howe and spoke in a whisper. "My Lord, you know this will come at a cost."

"Indeed," said the imp.

The creature raised its remaining taloned hand, and a column of fire shot high into the air. The flame arced and descended, landing on the stone floor and creating a magical bonfire. The villagers stopped and waited.

"This is a taste of what my master offers you," it said. "But it is not free."

It turned to Lord Howe. "Well? Do you accept what I offer?"

Lord Howe stared hard at the imp. "Power? Riches?"

"Eternal life," the imp added.

"What is the price?"

"Everything," the imp said. "You must admit it is a fair price for . . . everything."

Lord Howe heard footsteps behind him. He turned to see Lady Howe descending the steps.

"I've seen and heard enough," Sir Hugh said.

He stalked the imp, raising his sword.

"Stop!" Lord Howe said.

Sir Hugh froze, astonished.

"You cannot bargain with a demon, My Lord!"

The villagers shouted at the knights, eager to indulge in the new-found riches. The imp turned to Lord Howe.

"Well?" it asked.

Lord Howe's expression was unreadable under his devilish mask. He shifted on his feet. No doubt he struggled to decide.

"Hesitation is an answer, My Lord," the imp said.

Lord Howe staggered backward until he hit the wall. He reached for his mask, trying to take it off. He struggled. Everyone watched. No one moved to help.

The Marquess screamed as the mask undulated and twisted, becoming less a craft of paper maché and taking on the appearance of living flesh. Lord Howe fell to the floor and writhed in agony for only a few seconds.

When he returned to his feet, everyone gasped when they saw the mask had become Lord Howe's living face.

A heavy boom thundered through the castle and around the countryside. It rippled and echoed past the forest and the hills. The imp stood before the villagers. It gestured to the bonfire.

"Your costumes, your cloaks. All of your clothing goes into the fire until there is nothing left."

The villagers looked at each other, all of them too shy to be the first.

The coins vanished. The plates of food began to disappear one by one.

"When it's gone, it's gone for good," the imp said.

With that, the villagers ripped off their costumes and clothing. Lord and Lady Howe did likewise. In minutes, all were naked, watching their clothes burn in the fire. The food reappeared, and the coins dropped again in greater amounts. Tidal waves of gold. The villagers attacked the riches and began a hideous celebration.

Lord Howe raised his hand, and Lady Howe came to him. Her mask had likewise become her real face. The imp turned to the knights.

"The answer is no," Sir Berold said.

He raised his sword and the others did likewise.

"We will fight to the last."

"No need for that," Lord Howe said. "If you will not join, you are banished."

Sir Berold sheathed his sword. "You release us from our oaths to you, My Lord?"

"You are no longer bound to the Marquess of Ormond, my brave knights."

"Then we will seek Godly lands worthy of our swords," Sir Berold said.

The villagers paused their raucous indulgence as the knights left the great hall. Everyone followed to see them leave.

The knights raised the gate and lowered the drawbridge. The creatures outside remained. They watched with curiosity, their remaining instinct telling them something had changed within the castle walls. They parted the way for the knights.

"Look!" Sir Ralf said.

He didn't have to tell them. All the knights could see they had exited the castle to a wasteland. The spreading morning revealed ugliness and decay. The trees were twisted and bare. The grass was dirt. The sky was a mass of formless dark clouds. There was no color. Only gray.

"A grand bargain Lord Howe has made," Sir Hugh said.

The villagers followed them out and reacted in horror at the desolation that stretched out as far as they could see. Panic swept through the crowd. Lord and Lady Howe came out. The villagers begged them to undo the curse.

"What has happened?" Lord Howe asked the imp.

"I told you the price was everything."

Ignoring them, Sir Berold turned to his fellows. "Which way, brothers?"

"Let's go west," Sir Hugh said.

"Yes, the quickest way out of Lord Howe's kingdom of ashes," Sir Ralf said.

The knights laughed bitterly. They walked west, through the ruins of the village, past the dusty fields and into the thicket of dead, barren trees.

"Take us with you," a young woman from the village shouted.

As if in reply, the people began to twist and contort, screaming at the change their bodies went through. Limbs bent at unnatural angles. Hair and teeth fell out. Eyes lost their color and went black. Their voices lost the ability to form words. In minutes, the hissing, writhing mass of villagers looked no different from the strange creatures that arrived with the imp.

Lord and Lady Howe had not undergone the metamorphosis. They looked at their mutated subjects with distaste and fear. Lord Howe watched the knights grow smaller as they journeyed away, making their escape.

He looked at Juliana's new, grotesque face. The disgust in her eyes at the sight of his own devil face was apparent.

"At least we have each other, Juliana," he said.

She nodded.

"Let's return to our castle," he said, thinking of the food and drink and riches.

May as well enjoy what they have and bring their thoughts and attitudes in line with their new reality, the one they had paid for.

They turned to find the castle gone. There was only dirt and tree stumps where it once was. Two tree stumps sat side-by-side.

"Your thrones, Lord and Lady Howe," said the imp. "Sit and survey your—how did the knight call it? 'Kingdom of Ashes.' I like that."

Thunder split the sky again. Everyone looked up to see hundreds of icy spheres fall to the earth. The imp used his power of fire to melt the ice and free his demonic brothers. The other imps, after stretching and getting their footing, fell to instinct and assaulted the screaming mutants who once were hard-working peasants.

Their legs weak, the Howes dropped to the stumps and surveyed their "kingdom." The monstrous villagers wailed in torment from the attacking imps. Lord Howe stared into the distance with glazed eyes as the imp danced and sang and cackled to itself.

The four knights were gone.

James B. Christensen

The Giants of Rilara

As global disasters go, Rilara fared quite well. Most of the population had survived. The dead were counted mostly as those who refused to believe the prophecy, refused to be cautious, refused to evacuate the planet. Refused to live.

On the downside, everything they knew was gone. Cities, forests, ancient buildings, homes. All were swept away. They returned to Rilara, but it was a new planet as surely as if they had left the galaxy.

The prophecy of The Shift was part of Rilaran lore, remembered and preserved since the earliest days of their existence. The prophecy was delivered by Maarr, Lord of the Sky, the supreme deity of Rilara. His gigantic children turned against him in the final days, but they were never seen either. The legends of Maarr were silent on what became of them.

Although none had ever seen Maarr, his given words guided life on Rilara. For ages his prophecy passed down by firelight, father to son, mother to daughter. Most lived their lives with the prophecy in the background of their consciousness. The appointed time was simply too far away, long past anyone's expected death. With each generation, it became more of a reality.

The Shift referred to a rotation of the surface crust of Rilara. The surface would rotate over the planet's core as a peel would move over the fruit within. The frozen poles would become the warm tropics, and vice versa. Lands would submerge. Underwater realms would see the sun. The vast oceans would do what they do—find the path of least resistance and settle into oceans again, although with different shores. The time of The Shift had been part of the prophecy for as long as the prophecy existed. Not only was The Shift supposed to happen, the Rilarans even had the day given to them via the stated position of the stars and a series of celestial events—smaller predictions that, by virtue of having come true, added weight to the grand prediction of The Shift.

Maarr's prophecy further claimed that such a shift had happened before. Who could say how many times? It was possible such an event came around with regularity like spokes in the gears of a galactic watch. It was only by virtue of Maarr's intervention that a group of Rilarans survived the disaster to start again. He carried them to dry ground upon his vast wings, the legends said. He gave them a second chance along with a prophetic warning to prepare them for the next shift.

As the time of the prophesied shift drew closer, discussion of it became more earnest. Was it really going to happen? That question was argued from cities to farms. The High King and his subordinates pondered what to do. To prepare for The Shift and have it not happen would end up being a colossal waste of time, effort, and money. Such embarrassment might even undermine his rule. To dismiss the prophecy and take no action meant the eradication of their people if they were wrong. The High King decided he must act in faith toward Maarr's prophecy. To ignore the sky god's warning was to denounce all they believed in, the basis of their existence.

Still, there were powerful skeptics to satisfy, so in the name of peace the High King ordered an expedition to find any evidence of a previous shift. If it had happened before, as the prophecy claimed, then there should be some sign of it, somewhere.

A team of men and women both brave and smart set out to find such evidence. They scaled the tallest mountain in Rilara, Mount Pleen. The mountain was so tall and treacherous it had never been conquered. If it had once been underwater, the team reasoned, there would be indications of its submergence.

In the meantime, the High King assembled a brain trust in the capitol city to draw up plans for the mass evacuation of all Rilarans. Such an effort had to start at the ground up. Rilara had no space travel. Theories and small-scale experiments were as far as it had gotten. Once The Shift project moved forward, the brain trust got money and attention, then went to work.

The expedition's success at scaling Mount Pleen should have been cause for worldwide celebration on its own. It was overshadowed by its greater purpose. Shock and wonder swept the planet when the expedition returned with a frozen serpentine creature as long as ten men placed head to toe. Although it underwent the requisite inspections by teams of animal experts, anyone could see it was the preserved carcass of an ancient Yizzit serpent, named for the ocean where the frightening beasts made their home.

There was only one way a deep sea creature could end up on the world's highest mountain, and it wasn't via an expedition. The only conclusion was that the long-ago crust shift had indeed taken place, and that the shift had been so sudden that Mount Pleen, previously located at the north or south pole, had changed position so rapidly that the hapless animal had been snared by the moving mountain, tossed about by the raging waters, and stranded at the mountain's summit where the mountain ice imprisoned it.

With that discovery, the High King devoted more time and resources into the evacuation effort. The Temples of Maarr were full again. There were still pockets of disbelievers, but they were few.

Rockets were designed and refined. Orbiting satellites were tested and placed into orbit by the tens of thousands. They would house the fleeing citizenry and store up supplies. Anti-gravity hovercraft were developed for terrestrial exploration, to be used when The Shift was over and the waters settled around the new assortment of continents.

The great evacuation was an emotional moment for all Rilarans. For months the ships came and went, taking families and individuals, slowly removing the population and leaving those behind who refused to go. Evacuation ships filled the sky, an infinite hive of bees constantly in motion. The children enjoyed the excitement, caught up in the moment. The adults did their best to suppress their anxiety with optimism for the new world.

They evacuated Rilara a full month in advance of The Shift, just to be sure. Those were the dreariest days. Wondering and waiting in the cramped orbitals to see if it would really happen, and what, if anything, would be left for them to start over with.

When the time came, the orbiting ship commanders told residents to look out their viewing windows. Those who could bear the awesome sight gathered around to look down at their home world.

At first it was hard to detect any motion. Then someone pointed and shouted to look at the seas. The waves churned and swelled to terrifying heights. Everyone felt relief that the evacuation had happened. Mount Pleen and its surrounding continent of Vaa moved north, cutting through the raging oceans, splitting gigantic waves as it passed. Smaller islands and continents vanished forever. The waves continued to crash in mountains of white foam as the water violently searched for rest.

As Vaa moved steadily north, another continent followed Vaa from the south. Olinnis, the southernmost land long buried under miles of ice, crept behind its sister, likewise bashing against the undulating ocean. Following in Vaa's wake, the ice continent suffered a brutal battering by waves larger than any sailor's nightmare. The ocean pummeled away huge chunks and sheets of ice that fell to the waters to melt. People whispered prayers to Maarr, hoping he was still overseeing the welfare of Rilara.

When Olinnis had reached the equatorial zone previously inhabited by Vaa, the rotation stopped. The waters continued to swirl for weeks. Due to the disruption in water and currents, the weather went berserk, obscuring the view with spiraling dark clouds and lightning.

In time, the Rilarans grew bored with watching clouds and returned to the temporary lives they'd established in space. Speculation began again. All questions remained unanswered.

When the seas calmed, and the ocean temperatures and currents had stabilized, the clouds parted. People returned to the viewing windows.

True to the predictions of Rilara's best and brightest minds, Olinnis was the only land mass above sea level. All other lands were either underwater, or in the process of freezing at the poles for the next few thousand years. However, Olinnis was large enough to accommodate the returning population. That return would have to wait a little longer, though, as the heavy ice covering would take weeks to melt away.

Nothing about Olinnis was known for sure. Any details came from legend. It was a grand kingdom, according to the tales, a place of learning and innovation and great luxury. It was in the capitol city, Edes, that Maarr made his home and throne.

Conditions had settled enough that talk began to spread that a return trip to the surface was imminent. The High King took the opportunity to declare Maarr's greatness. The prophecy had come true at the year and time predicted. No matter what lie ahead, they could trust in Maarr's plan, and hope they would prosper in his future.

The first exploratory ships were sent down. Several tiny islands were discovered, but few were fit for habitation and would probably remain empty. Fleets of hovercraft circled Edes, the capitol city, which sprawled around the central mountains. The first reports were encouraging. The continent had wide plains to compliment its mountainous center. Several natural bays lined its outer shores. There would be room for everyone, and plenty of natural resources for all sorts of industry, trade, and farming.

The melt progressed quickly. The outer shores were already free of ice, but they were still uninhabitable due to the gushing water coming down from the melt like raging rivers. The increasing warmth of the continent heated the ice from within, causing great vertical cracks to split the mammoth sheets of ice. This caused a chain reaction of smaller cracks, which begat even smaller cracks, and on it went until heat and gravity sent avalanches of ice boulders tumbling down the central mountains of Olinnis and into the sea.

Hovercraft cameras broadcast the view to the ships above. People gasped in wonder at the majestic cities glowing in the sun for the first time in several millennia. The cities were not much different from the ones they had lived in. There were farm settlements here, villages there, port cities all around. All tragically empty.

An unexpected shock greeted the hovercraft pilots examining the base of the melt. Bodies of the long-ago dead, frozen for millennia, started to wash free from their icy tombs. The melting currents carried them across the plains toward the shore. At first it was one or two, but as the melt reached into the cities, the dead washed out by the hundreds, then thousands. Some swept off the continent where the sea claimed them again, but most collected on the shores in huge piles.

The High King consulted with his advisors and the lower kings to decide on a course of action. The obvious choice was to give each dead Rilaran a respectful burial. These were the mothers and fathers of Rilara, after all. However, the overwhelming numbers of dead rolling out from the melting continent made such a task impossible. It would take years to dig the graves and conduct the ceremonies. Such a large count of dead bodies had to be dealt with on an industrial scale, despite the respect they had for their ancestors.

They dug a great pit in a remote southern section of the continent to use as a burial site. The brain trust that designed and implemented technology for the evacuation got to work again, only this time to devise a plan to conduct tens of thousands of corpses into great fire pits where they were burned. Some bodies were collected for historical study, but most were dropped into the bay. Once that grim task was done, the pit was filled in, the souls of the dead consecrated to Maarr, and the site treated as a holy place to their people.

The High King announced this intention to the people. He promised he would beseech Maarr to bless this plan and forgive them their inability to deal with each dead Rilaran separately. Gloom settled over the people at the king's announcement, but they accepted it was the only way. The technical minds set to work as the bodies continued to gather. Hovercraft teams continued their observation and exploratory tasks, focusing on the high ground in the center.

The central mountains were a trio of equally tall peaks. In fact, the peaks were so alike that speculation ran through the orbiting colonies. What if they weren't natural formations? There were plenty who scoffed at such an idea. To carve mountains was a skill beyond even the bright minds that had put them into space. Still, people talked.

Due to its altitude into the cold thin air, the central peaks were the last to melt. By then the disposal of bodies had begun. Anti-gravity hovercraft lifted the bodies and dropped them into the pit. Although the hovercraft cameras broadcast the effort, not many people watched. By then, the three peaks provided a welcome distraction.

When smooth columns appeared through the shrinking ice among the three peaks, it caused such elation that the people insisted it was time to return to Rilara. Not only columns, but an entire vast temple network was revealed. Arches and turrets and spires, all made of gleam- ing white stone. All of a size made to accommodate beings much larger than the average Rilaran. In the center of the complex was a round temple with bridges and corridors leading away from it. Topping the center temple was an enormous round column stretched horizontally between two supports.

The grand temple of Maarr. Just as the legends had said.

While the people were elated at this validation of their faith, the High King and his council of kings huddled aboard his private ship to discuss the discovery. At issue was the size of the temple. In the old Rilara, there were certainly temples all over the land, and all were luxu- rious and elaborately decorated as tributes to the gods should be. How- ever, the old temples were not built with giants in mind. The halls and porticoes comfortably fit the average Rilaran. Maarr was Lord of the Sky. He did not live in the temple. His children, however, were despotic giants rebellious to their father's benevolent rule. The High King wanted to know—what did this mean? Was the grand temple built to conform to the giant tyrants? Who was in charge here?

He made sure his advisors knew he sought truth, not attempts to massage his ego. The discussion went in many directions. Some felt the oversized temple was the ancient Rilaran way of honoring the majesty of the Maarr. Others pointed out that little was known about the ancient days beyond the legends. Who knew the state of being? Maybe Maarr caused the earlier disaster to purge the planet of his rotten children, and now he had set things back the way he intended.

Frustrated at the lack of consensus, the High King once again commissioned an expedition to find the answers he sought so he could make an informed decision. The mighty, tri-peaked temple was almost totally free from ice and had been mapped out from the outside. The inner floor layout was unknown. The hovercraft had observed platforms and courtyards with plenty of space to allow a hovercraft or two to land.

Hovercraft pilots with the best performance ratings received the honor of joining the expeditionary force. They were given a week of relaxation with their families, then boarded their craft for the descent to the central mountains of Olinnis in the capitol city of Edes.

They circled the temple from the air. The ice had fully melted from the outside, leaving all the breathtaking contours and edges gleaming in the sun. Bridges and walkways joined the peaks across dizzying chasms. It was beyond anything a living Rilaran had seen or experienced. While the people were enthralled, the High King was uneasy. He knew how small he seemed next to this. Maybe the people didn't make the comparison right away, but when their surprise and wonder died down, they might.

Two hovercrafts landed in what looked to be the main courtyard. It spread out before the main building of the temple, which was an uneven, asymmetrical pile of cubes going this way and that, defying gravity and physics. The expeditionary team left the safety of the ships. Their boots splashed down into the melted ice water pooled on the courtyard's stone floor. Not in thousands of years had any living Rilaran walked these stones. Perhaps they had never done so. It was possible they were on holy ground forbidden to mere mortals.

If the team thought about such things, they put it aside and moved into the temple complex. They stepped through the main portico, trying to stop themselves from shaking as they beheld the vast, vaulted ceilings. Millions of brilliant white gemstones adorned the angled ceiling and refracted the entering sunbeams, spraying rainbow reflections on the walls, floors, and Rilarans.

Further on, toward the center of the complex, the ice still held. Distorted through clear ice, a hallway was visible. The team had prepared for this. A sub-group had already assembled a series of heat reflectors, courtesy of the brain trust. They positioned and angled the reflectors to direct the sunlight deep into the temple complex and melt the remaining ice. Hoses and pumps were ready to discard the resulting water. The contrast between machine and temple was a stark one. There was a period of waiting as the melting work was conducted.

Nightfall had descended by the time they declared the temple free of ice. Luckily, the twin moons of Rilara meant it was never truly dark. The team removed the melting equipment. The temple was back to its original state. Those glittering gemstones covering the ceiling and walls cast a soft yellow glow through the corridor. While the team was armed with pistols, they agreed to keep them holstered unless absolutely needed. If there were gods, what good would pistols do?

The wide main corridor continued straight though the temple complex. While smaller halls sprouted away at various intervals, the team kept the main one, knowing it took them closer to the center. Open windows cut into the walls and looked out to the bridges, peaks, and ocean beyond. An incredible sight. It also gave them an idea of their approach. When they could look out to see the round outer walls of the inner temple, they knew they were close.

A small vibration worked its way through the corridor. Each man and woman on the team felt it. At the end of the corridor, a splash of colored light illuminated the entrance. The team exchanged looks. This was the moment of reckoning. The leader informed the team that now was the time to retreat if anyone wanted to go back. They all decided to stay, and so they moved forward.

They entered the central temple and for a long moment could only stare. A wide, tall column stood in the center of the room. Six massive alcoves lined the column. Within each alcove was a giant frozen in ice. The giants were three times the size of an average Rilaran. The team circled the column. They were male and female like the Rilarans, and three of each gender were represented in the alcoves. Their skin was greenish blue, and their faces bore resemblance to certain sea creatures of the Yizzit ocean. The giants' limbs and expressions had frozen in seconds.

The sons and daughters of Maarr.

The team transmitted to the High King's ship to ask if they saw the beings. They received a generic yes. The team got an uneasy feeling the highest levels of power did not welcome the discovery.

People on the orbiting ships watching the discovery were silent. The children of Maarr were no legend. It was all real, no longer a matter of faith. They were the first of their kind in recent memory to *know*. It was a lot to process. They could only watch in silence. Maarr had appeared. The final state of things had yet to be known. If the giants were children of the sky god, they should have been immortal. How did they die? Others peculated they might be advanced beings instead of gods. Was there a difference?

The dead Rilarans washed free from the cities were a big enough challenge to deal with, and only because of the large numbers of them. How, the team wondered, were they supposed to deal with the bodies of giants? They were still frozen in ice, but in the tropics, even at this high altitude, the ice would melt soon. The brain trust would have to get to work again.

Word came down to the team to wait and watch while the High King deliberated with his advisors. So they waited. Once in a while they would examine the frozen bodies and their surroundings. Archaic symbols covered the column, along with writing nobody could decipher. The team busied themselves taking down details while casting nervous looks at the beings. Theories abounded as to what would happen now. Legends recounted tales of the giants' cruelty, and Maarr's resulting wrath.

Water pooled at the bottom of the column as the ice continued to melt. Gradually the giants' skin met the air. A forehead here, a knee there. The team's attention settled around the alcove with the most ostentatious decoration. A male, by the looks of him. By the level of ornate attention, probably the leader. Chief rebel. His forehead was exposed. The ice eased its way down his face until his nose and closed eyes were free.

Another inspection was made of the giants. It was agreed that the ice would soon weaken to the point it could no longer support the great weight of the creatures. They asked the High King for a decision.

Let them fall if they must, the King told them. The brain trust would figure out how to get them out and properly buried. All they could do was get out of the way if they were to let the giants fall, so they gathered their equipment and prepared to move out. Having one last glance before leaving the room, one of the team yelled at the others to look at the chief god.

His eyes had opened.

The team heard the shouts and cries from their superiors on the orbiting ships to get out. Once the giant's eyes opened, he broke through the remaining ice, his muscular arms stretching into the chamber. Ice cracked and smashed to the floor as the other giants broke free.

They stepped out of the alcoves with hard, thudding footsteps.

On the High King's ship, everyone shouted at once, clueless on what to do or how to confront the awakened gods.

The giants looked around as their senses returned. Recognition of each other passed through the group as they gathered by the leader. All of them stretched and shook off thousands of years of sleep.

None of the team members were able to move. They stood frozen in the same places they had been when the giants awakened. One by one, the creatures took notice of them.

The chief god walked to the team leader. The temple shook under his weight. The god asked how long they had slept. Speaking in a shaking voice, the leader told him the best guess was six thousand years.

Astonished looks covered the faces of the gods. They could hardly believe it had been so long. The giant asked the team leader if he was Rilaran. He answered yes. There was no denying it, and he had no deceptive answer if he meant to be something else.

Angered by this answer, the chief god grabbed the leader, left the center temple, and walked out onto a circling terrace. The hovercraft cameras watched him walk outside. The other gods followed, each carrying team members until every member of the squad dangled helplessly in a giant's grasp.

The chief god held the team leader over the terrace. He bellowed his demand for blood sacrifice and shouted his name, Sillu. His companion gods did likewise, and the Rilarans kicked their legs in terror, waiting to drop.

Weeping and wailing filled the orbiting ships. How could they return to Rilara under these circumstances? Sillu was ruler of Rilara now, so it would seem.

Several people on the High King's ship pointed out this fact. He ordered a hovercraft sent over to take him down to the planet. His advisors implored him not to go. He told them to ready the fleet to leave orbit if he couldn't fix the situation. Perhaps they could find a new world. That or death was preferable to life under this Sillu.

The High King stood before cameras and broadcast his plea for his countrymen to reach out with their minds and prayers to Maarr. As High King, he not only had a duty to confront any usurper to Rilaran rule, he was the flesh and blood representative of Maarr. It likely meant his death, but he vowed to go to his end with honor, if need be.

As they watched their king's ship depart, everyone went silent as they spoke to Maarr the Most High with whispers and thoughts, begging his return.

A distant thunder shook the hills and buildings. Sillu and his companions paused and looked around, for the first time seeming unsure and confused. They backed away from the edges of the temple. Thunder rolled harder. Thick, white clouds gathered in the east. The giants dropped their prisoners, and the Rilarans wasted no time running away and back to their hovercraft.

The giants watched them run away, and walked after them, still puzzled. The team boarded their craft and made their escape as the giants entered the courtyard, frowning at the flying ships. They had never seen Rilarans flying through the air before. They discussed this between themselves, trying to make sense of it.

People on the orbiting ships kept their concentration. If Sillu and the others were real, surely Maarr was also real and would hear them.

The High King landed on the courtyard where the expedition had earlier fled. The giants watched his approach. He studied them with growing dread. Distraction came easy to them. A hovercraft would draw their gaze this way, thunder would have them all look that way. Their eyes were cunning, yet childlike. Confusion made their anger boil. They stood before him, wondering what to make of a Rilaran who didn't flee from them.

He informed them he was High King of Rilara, Servant of Maarr. At the mention of the sky god's name, Sillu roared in fury. The High King knew he was surely dead.

A great shadow passed between Edes and the sun. The giants scanned the sky, this time truly afraid. Mighty wings spread wide, dwarfing the giants as it burst through the white clouds. It was a magnificent creature, a great silver and blue dragon with feathered wings, a scaled belly, and a terrible fanged face colored with wrath.

Maarr had returned. The High King stared in awe. He could only hope this was good news for him and his people.

The giants screamed and ran, but there are few places for a giant to hide. Maarr swept down and took Sillu first. Talons like tree branches dug into Sillu's flesh. Maarr carried him over the chasm and let him drop. The remaining giants, seeing Sillu's fate, alternately begged for mercy and cursed their estranged father as they tried to outrun him. He caught up to all of them. Soon the air surrounding the grand temple filled with the screams of the doomed giants. Whatever had happened between Maarr and his children, it was now settled.

Cheers and whoops of joy sounded throughout all the orbiting ships. Surely Maarr had come to let them live. The High King stood alone on the courtyard as Maarr descended to the horizontal column and sat upon it on his powerful hind legs.

The High King dropped to his knees. A voice penetrated his

thoughts, ordering him to stand. It was the voice of Maarr. He rose to his feet and faced the sky god. Maarr studied him for a few minutes, looking into his soul, his thoughts, his intentions. He told the High King to order the people's return, and the king did so.

All of Rilara returned to the surface to begin their lives anew. Maarr sat on his perch, watching his people organize their lives again. The High King took his office in a wing of the grand temple. Maarr would speak to him and answer questions as to the reorganization. For one month, Maarr watched the lands from his perch for all Rilarans to see and believe.

At the end of the month, Maarr summoned the High King and the people to assemble in the city of Edes. He sanctioned the king's rule, ordering him to always rule justly. Do so and he would have the sky god's favor. The High King pledged his loyalty to that command. The people of Rilara cheered their new life.

Maarr nodded, then flapped his great wings to rise high into the air. He flew to the east. And the rise of Rilara was complete.

James B. Christensen

The Tribunal

Two men dressed in black stepped off the boat and took a few seconds to regain their balance. Their journey had been fourteen hours of nature's fury. Not any random collision of cold and hot air fronts, but a malevolent act meant to prevent the two men from reaching their destination. That would sound crazy to the outside world, but the luxury of living in ignorance meant believing such things didn't happen. These two kept hidden knowledge so the world didn't have to live in fear of it.

First, the men endured a long journey by private aircraft. A category 5 hurricane rose up to assault the plane with such suddenness that weather forecasters around the world expressed their befuddlement. The two men riding in the battered plane, along with the trio of pilots, expected the hurricane.

After breaking into the eye of the storm, the pilots took advantage of the momentary calm to land on an isolated island. There, the two men in black piloted a small yacht to another island even further away from any civilization. The boat journey was just as treacherous as the one by air. The men navigated with faith and courage, certain that a protecting force was upon them, working against the invisible hands that sought to do harm. They remained steady at the helm, even as swells thirty feet and higher lashed down upon them.

Despite the ungodly weather working against them, the pair arrived on the tiny island on schedule. There was no mistaking they were at the right place. A high tower dominated the island, fortified by means both obvious—guard stations, fences, etc.—and not-so-obvious.

A squad of black-clad soldiers met the pair at the dock. They escorted the two men away from the dock and up to higher ground just as a wave crashed into the yacht, destroying it. The men and their guards looked back as the sea swept away the remnants of the boat. Commander Boyce, the leader of the squad, looked at the pair and grinned.

"I guess the boat doesn't enjoy divine protection," he said.

Mike, one of the two travelers, laughed. He seemed utterly unconcerned by the weather. "The prince is not a happy one today."

"His rage is impotent. Today is a victory for the armies of God," said Gabe, the second traveler. He carried a black duffel bag slung over his shoulder.

"Yeah, well, we're glad you're here," Boyce said. "This is the worst I've seen."

"That's saying something," Gabe said. "Considering your length of service."

"Some days I long for a return to conventional warfare, bad as it was."

Mike and Gabe laughed again. Jovial fellows they were. They knew Commander Boyce was only jesting.

A bolt of lightning struck one of the numerous lightning rods placed around the fortress.

"Best we get inside," Boyce said. "You've got a job to do, and we'd best not flaunt the Lord's protection."

They jogged the rest of the way up the hill to the fortress as the wind, rain, and lightning chased them along. The fortress flew no flag, had no name, no identifying signs or markers.

The group passed through several layers of security to enter the building. Retina, voice, and fingerprint scans. A blood sample analysis. At the last security check, each man had to pass through a mist of holy water.

After clearing security, the guards took Mike and Gabe to a room to change clothes and dry off.

"We'll be in the control room when you're ready," Boyce said.

The two men freshened up and changed in silence. It was best to remain with one's thoughts before the confrontation they were here to face. When ready, each man sat with his eyes closed—praying, meditating, thinking about the battle ahead. Whatever final preparations they thought were necessary.

Boyce stood at a one-way mirror when Mike and Gabe arrived. The room was a bustle of activity. Men and women worked at computers and consoles, keeping track of an endless array of readouts and information. The two men joined the commander.

The window looked down into a blood-splashed padded cell. In that cell, a large, terrifying man ranted and raved. He wore a white prison jumpsuit soaked in blood. Dozens of bullets had torn through his body and perforated his head. Despite these fatal wounds, the man stomped around the room, waving his tree-trunk arms and howling in an unholy rage.

"How did you catch this one?" Mike asked.

Commander Boyce sighed. "He was a toughie. Took us a year to catch on to his pattern."

"Where did he work?" Gabe asked.

"Mostly across Europe," Boyce said. "His methods of killing varied."

"That always makes it harder," Mike said.

"There were landslides, floods, animal attacks, all sorts of events that seemed random and unrelated," Commander Boyce said.

"But he was behind it all?" Mike asked.

"That and more," Boyce said. "It's all in the dossier. I'd tell you to remember that it's real and not a horror novel, but you know."

"What was his victim count?" Gabe asked.

"Eighteen thousand dead," Boyce said.

"Yowza," Mike said.

"By far the worst we've ever captured," Boyce said.

"If the outside world only knew what a true serial killer was," Gabe said.

"We lost three squads capturing him in France," Boyce said. "All the high-level exorcists in Europe were called in. It took their combined strength and skill to subdue him for the trip here."

"Thank God for them," Mike said.

"They're getting older," Boyce said. "We're not replacing them fast enough."

"It's under discussion," Gabe said. "It will be handled. Now, about this one. I see he's been executed."

The men laughed.

"Oh yes," Boyce said. "He was found guilty by the tribunal. I'd estimate the firing squad put forty-two rounds into him."

"And still he rages," Mike said.

"It's the demon that survives," Boyce said.

"What do we know about the man?" Gabe asked.

"Istvan Benyo is his name," Boyce said. "Hungarian. In regular life just an average man who worked hard and drank hard. But he had a dark side. We uncovered links to the Zortis cult."

"Which is how this possession happened," Mike said.

"A pretty safe bet," Boyce said. "In fact, the entity within Mr. Benyo is so powerful we believe the demon is Zortis himself."

Mike and Gabe were shocked.

"That's the consensus of the exorcists?" Mike asked.

"Unanimous."

"Then you were right to call us," Gabe said.

"I hope your powerful friend cooperates," Boyce said. "Because this is a bad one."

"Angels are unpredictable, but our friend knows the stakes," Mike said.

"And knows he has an enemy and who it is," Gabe said.

"That's fortunate," Boyce said. "It's also fortunate that Zortis is as arrogant as he is. He thought he could resist the ordained power of the exorcists. He almost did. However, had he simply fled the body, he would be free to find another."

"Obviously the execution did not expel him," Gabe said.

"Which is why you're here," Boyce said. "If we can contain this demon, we'll have struck a powerful blow for good."

"If he gets away, more will suffer and die than before," Mike said.

They watched the man who was Istvan Benyo as he pounded the walls.

"We're ready whenever you are," Boyce said.

The demon-controlled corpse ceased its rantings and looked up at the window, which was a mirror from its point-of-view. The bloodied, contorted face broke into a wide, satanic grin.

Mike and Gabe exchanged a look, reading each other's expression.

"Yep, I see you're ready," Boyce said.

Boyce led them through a series of corridors and to a secure elevator.

"You know the drill, fellas," Boyce said. "The east-facing wall of the cell opens to the outdoors. You are all that stands between the demon and his escape. We have to open to the outside because that's how your unpredictable friend requires it."

"We've tried to change his mind, believe me," Gabe said.

"You two have a good track record," Boyce said. "I hope it continues."

"Well, in case of a bad outcome, it's been nice working with you," Mike said.

Boyce laughed. "All we can do is give Him our best. If it results in death, well, it is just a doorway."

The elevator descended to the ground floor and opened up to another corridor that ended with a fortified door with a squad of soldiers guarding it. Together, Boyce and the soldiers went through the painstaking process of opening it.

Sheets of rain greeted the group as the soldiers opened it wide. Everyone stayed behind as Mike and Gabe walked a path around the outer wall where a rectangular line set into the wall indicated a door.

Gabe set his duffel on the ground and took out a ceramic jar. The clamped lid was etched with a six-sided star formed by two inverted, overlapping triangles. A circle surrounded the star.

The two men knelt to pray.

"This container is made from the Earth of your creation, oh Lord, mixed with the ashes of your precious martyrs, and sealed with the symbol of your servant King Solomon," Gabe said.

"Give us strength, almighty God, against the forces of darkness," Mike said. "We beseech thee to send your terrible angel to aid us in your cause."

Together, they said, "But let not our will, but thine, be done. Amen."

By now, Commander Boyce had returned to the control room, and watched the two men by surveillance camera. He watched them open the ceramic jar and hold it ready. They looked up at the security camera and signaled.

"They're ready," Boyce said to a subordinate at a computer. "Lower the outer wall."

The control room went deathly silent. Boyce returned to the one-way mirror and watched the demon-possessed man. He looked around, puzzled, at the rumble of the lowering wall. When he realized what was happening, he grinned that awful grin once more and turned to face the revealing storm, anticipating his escape.

Outside, Gabe and Mike exchanged a final look before the wall completed its descent into the ground.

"I hope I'm worthy," Mike said.

"I hope you're worthy, too," Gabe said. "Otherwise, this will be messy for both of us."

The men laughed. Laughter was the best defense against the terror they regularly faced.

The wall was gone. The two men faced into the white padded cell. Zortis walked arrogantly toward them.

"Stand aside," he said with contempt.

The two men stood firm and straight.

"Fools! I've drunk the blood of thousands of your kind. You think I'll hesitate, men of God?"

"I'm sure you know killing us will be no easy task, Zortis," Gabe said. "You might. You might not. There is a risk to you as well."

Zortis roared. *"Arrogant, stupid, humanity! Image of God, my ass. I'll taste your sweet blood in seconds."*

"Best you flee the body now," Gabe said. "What's stopping you?"

"All in good time, Gabriel. Perhaps I'll take your body when I leave this ruined one?"

"You know better than that, demon," Mike said. "You are far from any sympathetic followers. Your worshipers have been eradicated. You are alone."

"I am more than enough!"

The demon opened its mouth, its jaw hinging wide to reveal rows upon rows of sharp teeth. It roared at the two men. If they felt any fear in their hearts, they kept it hidden. Zortis looked uncertain, obviously not used to this level of resistance.

"You only think my followers are gone. I have many you do not know about. Even now, they are violating the women and children of your line. Fools!"

"You are indeed a servant of the Father of Lies," Gabe said.

Gabe rose into the air, startled. Zortis shook with malicious laughter.

"Scared of heights, Gabriel?"

Now Mike lifted into the wind and rain. The two men swirled around each other while the Zortis roared with demonic glee. He let the two men drop. They hit the ground hard with a grunt. Gabe gasped in pain at his broken arm.

Zortis rushed forward, his awful fanged jaw wide open, and screamed in Gabe's face. Undead spittle covered the man's face, but he remained determined, his teeth clenched against the pain of his broken arm. Zortis kicked the arm. Gabe cried out, but still did not give in to fear.

Mike got the same treatment, getting a nose-to-nose scream from the creature. It picked him up by the arms.

"Two broken arms for you, I think."

Mike grimaced against the coming pain. Zortis squeezed Mike's forearms. Before he could twist them into a break, a wind stronger than the hurricane force howled across the island. The gust blew Zortis and the two men into the cell. All of them shook off the dizziness of the blows.

In the control room, Boyce watched it all, anxious.

Zortis staggered to his feet as the men remained on the floor. He froze when he looked outside.

There, a nine-foot tall specter cloaked in a long, tattered black hooded robe blocked the escape. Its face—if it had one—was in shadow. The wind did not sway it a bit.

Zortis stared at the newcomer, uncertain.

"Master?" he asked.

Gabe and Mike laughed. Zortis whirled on them in anger.

"Idiot demon," Gabe said. "That is not your master."

"It is not an angel of the Lord, fool!"

"Then by all means, take its hand and stroll away," Mike said.

Zortis stared at the apparition. The more he stared, the more horrified realization crept into its savage face.

"Death! The Angel of Death!"

"You only get to meet him one time," Gabe said.

The Angel of Death rushed into the room with terrifying speed and the screams of countless lost souls. Gabe and Mike got to their feet and staggered out of the room and out into the rain.

Zortis screamed, helpless, as the towering angel cornered him in the room. The death angel reached out a gnarled hand to the demon. The force released from the angel struck the body that once belonged to Istvan Benyo. Scraps of flesh and bone splattered away from the body like a spray of water hitting dirt. The creature screamed in fear.

Mike picked up the ceramic jar and held it ready.

When Benyo's body was no more, a formless red mist circled the padded cell. It feigned this way and that, but the Angel of Death would not let if pass. The angel turned to the two men.

"Our turn," Mike said.

Together, they held up the ceramic jar. The red mist twirled and stretched as if resisting a magnetic pull from the jar. After a long, mournful scream—a scream the men had heard many times—the mist vanished into the jar. When the last of it had been pulled in, Mike clamped the lid shut.

The storm abruptly ceased. The clouds cleared and let through the sun. The Angel of Death was gone. There was only Gabe, Mike, and the scattered remains of Istvan Benyo.

Commander Boyce and a team of soldiers trotted into the padded cell. Boyce looked around at the incredible scene.

"God be praised."

"The victory is His," Mike said.

"Let's get your arm fixed," Boyce said to Gabe.

"First things first, Commander," Gabe said.

Boyce nodded. "Very well. Follow me. You know the way, I guess."

He led them back to the secure elevator. Again the elevator went down, only this descent took several minutes, going deeper and deeper until they were far below the level of the ocean floor. When at last they came to a stop, they stepped out into a series of dim corridors.

Armed men in black staffed the area. They nodded and saluted as Boyce led the two men through. Another victory. Word had spread fast.

It took thirty minutes to clear their way through the most secure door in the world. Scans and traps and repetitive tests made sure only the most absolutely qualified entered through.

Boyce, Mike, and Gabe entered a warehouse. It stretched away until the far end faded into darkness. The warehouse was lined with shelves that reached to the ceiling, three stories above. The network of shelving was so vast Boyce had to drive them to their designated shelf via Jeep.

When they came to the specified shelf. Mike placed the ceramic jar on an empty space next to other similar jars.

As Boyce drove them back to the warehouse door, the two men stopped to appreciate the magnitude of what the room represented. Every inch of the miles and miles of shelves were filled with ceramic jars marked with the seal of Solomon.

The Architect

I can see the world from my front door. That's no exaggeration. When I step onto the wrap-around porch of my humble house—with its waist-high-safety railing—I'm greeted by the curve of planet Earth, the farmlands and forests, the ocean and the rivers that feed into her.

It's risky for a man my age to live so high. Not only is it a long way down should an old codger like myself take a tumble, but the air is thin. My family makes a habit of imploring me to move to a lower level. I still have enough strength to keep my balance. I rarely engage in activities that quicken my breathing. So for now, I'm satisfied to stay where I am. I enjoy the whistle of the wind at this altitude. The passing clouds make themselves at home, coming through the windows and filling my house with a ghostly fog. Clouds make it difficult to see the ground far below. Not only is the ground out of sight, I haven't walked on the soil of Earth in two decades. I'm a man of the sky. This wasn't always so.

I think in my twilight years about the changes I have seen. My grand-father, who thankfully didn't live to see what his descendants would go through, talked about war and change of governments and advances in science. Lots of change did he see—some of it worthwhile, some destructive. In balance, life became faster, more efficient. Again, good and bad came with that, but he was long gone to his final reward when The Blobs came.

You can chuckle, but that's what we called them at first, named for the old movie. I was twelve when a cruise ship sighted the first one in the Pacific Ocean. Hundreds of passengers and crew saw an amorphous blob floating in the sky, a bright blue mass the size of a small house, a large-scale version of those globules that float in lava lamps. Dismissed as mass hallucination, of course. But they kept showing up. Over land and sea. Over every country and ocean. They never touched the ground. They seemed to prefer keeping a certain distance above whatever mountain, skyscraper, or plain they observed. The Blobs followed planes and ships, hovered over sporting events and made their way over the tallest mountains and trees.

The powers that be saw no point in lying about their existence by then. At first there was no problem. Small-scale panic here and there. Predictions of apocalypse came and went. The Blobs didn't communicate. Self-appointed messengers claimed psychic connections. None of their predictions or pronouncements came true nor were they taken seriously. The only thing they communicated was a sense of innocent curiosity.

Just as people got used to their presence, even viewing them as benevolent pets, the attacks came. It was the house next door to mine. There was a party. I forget the occasion. By providence, I was not invited. I was outside with friends, intending to play baseball. Instead we stretched out on the ground to look up at the Blobs. By now they dotted the skies as far as we could see. A bright blue one floated to a position above the party house, then descended to twenty feet above the roof.

"What's it doing?" my friend, Billy, asked.

I watched people streaming into the house. I tried to picture what the Blob saw from its bird's-eye view. Like ants flowing into an anthill, I supposed. By then we knew The Blobs could see, based on how it followed and took an interest in people, animals, and natural features. Exactly how it saw things without eyes, we didn't know.

"Watching people go into the house, I guess," I said.

"That's it?" Michael, another friend, said. "They came from their home planet just to watch us all walk around?"

"I'm okay with that," Billy said.

"Me, too," I said. "What do you want them to do? Start shooting their lasers?"

That last question still haunts me. On cue, a thick, jagged bolt of red lightning erupted from the blob and tore into the house. People ran screaming as the house burst into flames. The three of us leapt to our feet and ran, looking back to see the red lightning striking down individuals on the run. The Blob didn't stop the lightning strikes until everyone in or fleeing from the house was a skeletal cinder.

We lived in fear after that. The attacks happened worldwide and continued for days and weeks, stretching into months and years. There was no rhyme or reason. The attacks would cluster within an hour, then spread out over days, then one per day for weeks. At first it was impossible to go on with life. Fear addled my brain. There was no escape. Billy and Michael were killed, along with their families. When people retreated underground, the Blobs found a way to bring water from the rivers and lakes, sucking it up from the surface and pouring it into the subterranean quarters, killing everyone.

This happened all over the world. Millions died. At least, that was the rough estimate when communications went down, along with all other infrastructure. The ease of transportation and communication on which we'd come to rely was gone. There were not enough people to maintain it. We had to resort to hunting and gathering. Anything that couldn't be repaired was left to rot or rust.

The large cities were hardest hit. Obviously they had more people, but the word spread while communications still functioned that one pattern to the attacks had been identified—The Blobs liked to strike at gatherings of people. Even small groups attracted their wrath.

So we became loners. Spreading out, never gathering in sight of the blobs, and communicating with Morse code through tapping wood and flashing lights. Even that was no guarantee of safety. The Blobs started picking out lone people here and there. Hiding in the woods was dangerous, as the animals aggressively dealt with their own culling by the Blobs. It was a way of life for attacks to happen at any minute. Someone you knew one day would be dead the next. You'd see friends, loved ones, strangers, seared by the awful red lightning at all times.

Over time, the constant, crippling fear gave way to acceptance. Although we still avoided gathering in groups, we resumed our daily lives as best we could. Walking down the street and seeing someone zapped became the new normal. It was acceptance or insanity. Although plenty went down the path of madness, most of us accepted death as a constant companion. Screams. Explosions. Fires. Terror. It was an everyday part of life. The end could come for anyone at any-time. It spurred people to authentic living, I can assure you. There was no time to waste. No way to know if a fight with your spouse would be the last words you would share, if a harsh word to your child would be the last they ever heard from you. We were kinder, more brave, doing our best to maintain what we had with dignity. We lost sight of how we had given up on creating a future.

It was my last year as a teenager when the Architect arrived. People had stopped traveling by then. The Blobs liked to attack "migratory routes," so people stayed put. So when the Architect came strolling down main street, carrying a large backpack, he was noticed. Like everyone else, he took it in stride when a woman telling him hello was incinerated by the red lightning.

Someone asked his name and business from a window as he walked by. He said he was an architect. He didn't want to give his name, so we called him by his profession.

He walked through the streets and out past the city limits. We were all desperate to follow him, thinking this might be some kind of deliv-erer, someone with a solution, but to follow as a group was suicide. We carefully made our way from building to building, watching him from windows. Some buildings were torched as the Blobs took notice of unusual activity. Still, we followed him until he came to a wide plain between the city and the forest. No one went out into the plain. It was grassland and humans stood out, which made them easy targets for the blobs. Yet he was fearless. We watched him from the windows of the buildings at the edge of the city.

Moving quickly and confidently, the Architect opened his backpack and withdrew several large strobe lights. He placed first one then another, setting the lights off so they flashed in red, blue, and white. It was dusk. The strobes were almost too bright to watch.

Several blobs moved over to the plain. The natural assumption was that the Architect was about to die, but something was different. He came here from another place, moved and acted with confidence.

With great care he paced out a certain distance before setting another strobe light. As expected, a bolt of red lightning struck a strobe light, leaving it in ashes. We ducked away from the windows, but the Architect kept about his business.

A shadow passed overhead. Another Blob had arrived, but this one differed from any we had so far seen. It was twice as large, and its color was more dark and muted compared to the usual bright blues, reds, and yellows. A smaller Blob struck out at a second strobe, and the large Blob struck the smaller one with yellow lightning. The smaller Blob shrank away.

An attack between The Blobs was something new. The Architect paused his light placement to look up at the large Blob, which hovered thirty feet above, as if watching him. He looked down from the large Blob and smiled at the buildings, knowing we watched him.

"Come out, friends," he said. "They will not attack again if you do as I tell you."

I looked around at the people in my building. Too much terror for too long. No way was I going out into that plain with an even larger Blob standing watch.

"They won't wait for too much longer," the Architect said. "If they see us working on the project I have for you, they will not attack. Keep them waiting too long, they will destroy everything."

"How do you know?" someone shouted from a neighboring building.

The Architect kept busy with his lights. Another giant Blob had arrived.

"I learned the hard way," the Architect said. "Things are changing. Total destruction will come to those who do not act. Come, my friends. Help me or die."

"Are we safe to come out?" someone asked.

"They kill us in groups!" said another.

"Not this time, they won't," he said.

I realized then how insane life had become. How I and everyone else had been reduced to pure animal survival. There was no thought to learning, innovation, love or family. Two girls I fancied had been killed by the Blobs. The idea of marriage and children was obsolete. I was among the last generation if things continued along this path. Was this how I wanted to continue? Crawling along to be the last living human to reach the finish line?

Die or do something different. I ran down the steps of the building and out the front door, along the street leading out of town and into the plain. The expected flash of pain and fire to end my life didn't come. The smaller Blobs undulated in the sky, agitated and anxious to cook my flesh, but the two large Blobs kept order. My confidence grew. By the time I reached the smiling Architect, I knew I would survive.

"Why aren't they killing you?" I asked.

He laughed at my choice of a first question. "Because I'm interesting to them."

"How?"

He gestured at the lights.

"That's all?" I asked.

"Not hardly, but it's a start," he said.

"What do you want us to do?" I asked.

"We're going to make something beautiful," he said.

People ran up behind me. All of us kept our eyes on the sky. It was a supreme act of faith to do this, knowing by hard experience what happened when we gathered in the open. The smaller Blobs twisted and churned, but did not attack. One of them flickered and glowed—a sign of coming lighting—but a larger one absorbed it before it could fire. The other smaller ones settled down.

"It wants to see what we'll do, right?" I asked.

"Yes," he said. "Best not to disappoint them."

First, he sorted us into groups, then had us walk from strobe to strobe in different patterns, flattening the grass with our shoes as we did. He had other groups go into the woods and fell trees, but only in a specific patterns.

After we struck the patterns in the grass, he instructed us to dig a foundation along the pattern while others hewed trees into boards.

"I went outside after they killed my family," the Architect said. "I hoped to get zapped and join them. None of those things took an interest in me. They just floated as if they were bored.

"So I took a walk. I thought if I moved around one of them would take me out."

He shook his head.

"I just kept walking. In a few minutes I came across a trail of ants. My first thought was to stomp and swipe them with my shoes. Ain't that funny? Like I was some 6-year-old."

"I used to do that, too."

"I didn't kill them. I followed them. I had nothing else to do. They went into the woods. I lost them a time or two, but I picked them up again and they led me to a clearing."

He was quiet. His eyes looked back through time.

"What did you see?" I asked.

"Ant hills."

"Oh."

"About twenty feet tall."

"What?"

He smiled and nodded. "As big as a house. Ants crawling all over it. No idea how long it took to do. I imagine it's the equivalent of humans making a skyscraper that reached miles and miles into the sky."

I looked around at the people digging and building and put it together.

"Standing there, I thought of my impulse of a few moments before," he said.

"To kill the ants?"

"Yes. And looking at that towering ant hill I was awestruck, humbled. No way would I have made any attempt to destroy something so beautiful."

"They see us as ants?" I asked.

"Seems as good a theory as any," he said. "I continued through the forest and to the beach where I tracked designs in the sand, as big and complex as I could manage. The large ones gathered, just as these have."

"They want to see what we'll do. See if we amuse them."

"Best not to let them get bored," he said.

He put his arm around me and led me back to the people in the field.

"I'll show you all the basics, then I'll move on, spread the word," he said. "Create beauty as if your life depended on it. Because it does."

That's how towers began. A deep foundation in the field, then the structure rose from the ground. Not just straight angles and boxy design. It curved and looped and leaned at impossible angles. The Architect taught us how to carefully balance weight, adjust to wind. The foundation sprouted out like a maze. He had us paint it with colorful murals. Jewels and metals and anything else that sparkled and reflected in the sun adorned its walls. When the project was well underway, when enough men and women were schooled in what needed to be safely done, the Architect said his goodbyes and moved on to spread the word further.

Higher and higher towers went. We moved in. We married and had children, me included. Then there were grandchildren. Our job was to build and expand. Construction took us to dizzying heights. Transport systems brought up food, water, and supplies from the ground. Rainwater was collected. Walkways connected the sprawling extensions of the towers, and one could walk around for acres in the sky without ever touching ground.

Indeed, some of us have children who have never been to the ground. Those of us who lived through the first attacks of The Blobs have an uneasy superstition of the ground. We prefer to stay away from it. It's an unspoken understanding.

Through all of this, The Blobs all but left us alone. There was an occasional attack by the small, more immature Blobs, but the larger ones retaliated so swift and severe that they learned their lesson. After that, they only watched our progress. We sensed approval and even delight in how they hovered and undulated as we progressed.

I tell my grandchildren this incredible tale. They hear the stories of my grandfather, just to put it all into the context of strange twists and turns life can take. Naturally, they want to know the changes they can expect in life. What's the end game, Grandpa?, they ask.

I don't know. Recent meetings among the governing council of the towers have been disconcerting. We're running out of ways to expand, they say. If we keep going, the integrity of the entire tower complex could collapse. But how will The Blobs react if the building stops?

The end could come at any time at my age. It's my family I worry about. How long does one have to live before they're considered a part of history?

There's no time for much philosophy, though. As I write, there is excitement swirling outside. People rushing toward one of the tallest center towers. I made my way up to see it, and came back to my journal.

It seems one of the large Blobs separated into smaller ones. They descended to the tower platforms and elongated to the height of an average man. They shape-shifted further until they had arms and legs, hair and eyes. The solid colors they had before changed into a perfect copy of human pigment of different races. In minutes, one could not tell one of these blob fragments from a real human.

This caused a volatile mix of elation and suspicion. I don't know what to make of it. I suppose things will play out as they will no matter my feelings for it.

Long ago I grew too old for the labor of the towers, but there is no retiring from the turns of history.

James B. Christensen

The Gate of Hanngee

Zia plopped into the cockpit seat with a sigh. Bria sat in the chair next to her. The sparkling vista of space spread out eternally in all directions through the windows. The steady hum and vibration of the engines kept them relaxed.

"Anything?" Zia asked.

"Just the stars," Bria said. She looked depressed.

Zia leaned back in her chair and gazed out the bridge windows of the small spacecraft.

"So beautiful it makes my heart ache," she said.

"They're always in the distance," Bria said. "The stars. The planets and whoever might live there. All of it. Back home I learned of the bigness of space. I had no idea until I was in the middle of it. Everywhere we go is emptiness. All this beauty beyond our grasp forever."

She turned to face Zia.

"We're the center of the universe wherever the ship takes us. Who knew the center was such a lonely place?"

"I like it," Zia said. "It's better than how things were at home, when we left. All those explosions and noise. People screaming. Fire in the air as we flew out. That's enough excitement for one lifetime for me."

"Is that a hint that I should shut up?" Bria asked.

Zia smiled, tired. "No. Just my opinion. I'm at peace."

Bria studied Zia. She shook her head, not understanding how Zia could be at peace.

Zia stretched and rubbed the sleepiness out of her eyes. The two women were on helm watch. There wasn't much to it. Mik, the skilled pilot of the group, had the spacecraft on autopilot. He had done the hard job of getting them off the planet during the conflagration of an unknown alien attack. Zia closed her eyes remembering how Mik had deftly steered the ship into the stars and through the wobbling stargate that drifted beyond the moons, right where Rak said it would be. The stargate spat them out into a separate, unknown galaxy. Into this eerie void. Rak and Mik were in their extended sleep capsules. In two hours, it would be time for the men to take over.

"Thanks for breakfast, by the way," Zia said.

"My pleasure," Bria said. "Opening those food cakes is hard work. I slaved for hours."

Zia laughed, mostly in surprise that Bria had a sense of humor.

"Well, you wanted peace and quiet, you have it," Bria said. "Sensors are still. Any planets are too far away to reach in our lifetime. If there are other stargates, we don't know of them. We should start new family trees. Who would you pick? Mik or Rak?"

Zia blushed. "It's possible other people from our planet escaped."

"Changing the subject," Bria said. "Besides, we've been a year 'at sea' with no contacts."

"Maybe we have family who survived," Zia said.

"Not me."

Zia winced. "Sorry. That was insensitive of me. I forgot."

"Don't worry about it," Bria said. "At least I know. Sometimes I think that's better than wondering."

Zia nodded and didn't respond. No need to make it a competition.

"What if we're the last of our kind?" Bria asked.

"Then we'll draw lots for Mik and Rak?"

Bria laughed, and the tension left in silence.

Zia rubbed her bare shoulders and looked out the bridge windows to the magnificent, unreachable vista.

"Cold?" Bria asked.

Zia shook her head. Like the others, she wore undergarments around the ship. Cooling the air took energy they couldn't spare, and there was no point in pulling on the flight suit.

"I like the heat," Zia said. "Keeps me sleepy. I'm so jumpy."

"Shellshock," Bria said. "Understandable."

"It's so peaceful out here. I don't know if I want to go anywhere else. Just sit and watch the stars."

"And eat."

"And drink."

"And start a family with Mik," Bria said.

Zia gasped and giggled. "So you're picking Rak?"

"You can have them both," Bria said.

Zia frowned at the dark tone Bria used. Bria was hard to understand.

Zia stretched her leg and worked the sensor controls with her toes, switching between different sensor arrays. Using her feet allowed her to stay reclined in the cockpit chair, half asleep. Training her toes to function as fingers helped pass the time. Bria watched Zia's dexterous feet in uncharacteristic silence.

The invaders who came to Bria and Zia's home planet were unknown and unseen. They came in great ships with terrible weapons and sought only to destroy. To what end, nobody could say. It was only the others' friendship with Mik that ensured their survival. As far as they knew, each of them, like Bria, were the dead end of their family line unless they could find a place to start over and see what might happen. Zia wondered if that was a bad thing.

A soft beeping snapped them to an alert state of mind. Bria sat up as Zia's toes flipped switches, pressed buttons, and turned dials. They interpreted readouts on a bank of screens.

"It's a signal," Bria said.

Their hearts beat faster than they had since their escape. The sensors had been quiet all this time.

"Good news, bad news, or just a bunch of nothing?" Bria asked.

Now Zia's hands took over, typing on the keyboard and entering commands, analyzing the signal.

"It's coming from port side. Far away," Zia said.

In minutes, they heard bare feet padding in the small corridor behind them. They knew it was Mik. Any anomaly picked up by his ship's sensors would automatically wake him up.

"What is it?" he asked.

He appeared on the bridge in his wrinkled undergarments.

"A signal," Bria said.

"Is there a message in it?"

"We've analyzed it every way we can think of," she said. "It's just a beacon."

He nodded. "Our first signal. Let's check it out."

"Could be anything," Bria said. "A wayward satellite. A marker. A piece of junk."

Zia gave up her seat to Mik. He checked the sensor readout and shifted the craft's trajectory toward the signal.

"Should I wake Rak?" Bria asked.

"Sure. It'll break up the monotony for all of us, if nothing else."

Mik laid in a new course and goosed the engines, making for the source of the signal. Bria returned with Rak. Everyone was alert and awake. Excitement crackled in the air. The rumbling engines heralded discovery. All of them knew better than to get their hopes up, but it couldn't be helped.

"Signal, huh?" Rak asked. "Anything yet?"

"A beacon," Mik said. "Not sure what's sending it."

"What do you think it is?" Bria asked.

"Space junk," Zia said.

"More alien ships with big guns," Bria said.

Zia frowned, but everyone remained silent, knowing Bria had suffered the worst escape.

"Let's have some optimism, maybe?" Mik said.

"He's right," Rak said. "If there's good energy we can draw it to ourselves."

Zia looked at them with a frown.

"Could be it's someone or something that can help us," Mik said.

The others watched him.

"Help us back home, I mean."

No one wanted to point out the high odds of anything coming to the aid of their destroyed planet.

The ship rumbled as the engines increased speed.

"Any readout yet on the source of the signal?" Bria asked.

"That's the weird thing," Mik said. "I've pinpointed the source, but there's nothing there."

"Nothing?" Rak asked.

"No ship. No planet. No object or structure of any kind. Just empty space."

"So it's coming out of nowhere?" Zia asked.

"Hey, computers don't lie, right?" Mik said.

"How long 'til we reach it?" Rak asked.

"At this speed, another hour."

"Well, I say we eat something," Bria said.

Everyone looked at her.

"Might be our last dinner," she said. "Let's enjoy."

Mik sighed. "Enough, Bria. We'll eat, but let's pass on the cynicism, okay?"

Bria shrugged and left for the galley. "It's not like we'll be on this thing forever either way."

They tried not to think of the end game, should the ship never find a friendly port.

"Hey, whatever makes the time go by," Rak said. "*Something's* sending the signal. I can't wait."

"In that case, let's not drink too much," Mik said.

The cramped galley was just big enough for the four of them. They crowded around the table and enjoyed flavored food cakes. To them, it was a feast. They took turns returning to the bridge to track their approach of the signal.

"Okay," Mik said. "Let's speculate. What's sending the signal?"

"I think it's another ship," Rak said. "I think there's opportunity coming."

Zia cut her cake with a fork held in her toes. "I hope it's nothing. This is the part of space I like. Nothing."

"You don't go far enough, Zia," Bria said. "I think we've been chased. I think the end of the world didn't like us getting away, and now it's coming to finish the job."

Mik cleared his throat. "Bria, I know what happened to your family, but it probably happened to our loved ones, too."

"You didn't have to see them die. Besides, you don't know that. They could still be alive. Maybe you abandoned them."

"This provocation won't work," Mik said. "We're here, and that's the way it is. Now, my question: can I trust you to care for this ship when it's your watch?"

"I couldn't self-destruct it anyway," she said.

That didn't make anyone happy.

"Morbid joke. Sorry," she said. "I'm not a killer or a saboteur."

Mik seemed satisfied with that. Bria watched him, wondering what he might have done had she given the wrong answer.

"How 'bout you, Mik?" Rak asked. "What are you hoping to find?"

Mik chuckled softly. "Something ridiculous. Something so impossible only a fool would dare hope for it."

"What?" Zia asked.

"A miracle. A super weapon or a giant ship of benevolent beings who will come to our aid and help us reclaim our planet."

Everyone ate and drank quietly, trying not to show their irritation with Mik for bringing hope into the equation.

"Now I'm the one who's sorry," Mik said. "I'm setting my hopes too high. Stupidly so. I realize that. I just feel an obligation. I'm the military man of the group, and I fled."

"You *rescued*," Zia said. "Us. You did your duty."

Mik nodded. After a quiet moment, he left to return to the bridge.

"I don't care what it is," Bria said.

Mik's voice came over the intercom, telling everyone to come to the bridge. They arrived to find Mik in the cockpit with a puzzled look.

"Want to see what's making the signal?" Mik asked.

Everyone gathered around Mik and peered out the windows.

"I don't see anything," Bria said.

"Where is it?" Rak asked.

Mik pointed. "Right in front of us."

Zia sighed. "There's nothing there. Stop playing. What's going on?"

"Look at the readout," Mik said.

The others pressed in to see.

"According to this, the signal's coming from right in front of us," Mik said. "About twenty yards, I'd say."

Rak squinted. "Nothing there. Is it invisible? Cloaked?"

"I've scanned and re-scanned," Mik said. "Empty space."

"What if the signal's coming through another portal?" Bria asked.

"Would have to be a small one, but it's possible," Zia said.

They stared into space for a moment. The signal light continued to flash, defying their own eyes.

"Let's go out and have a look," Rak said.

Mik studied him. "You really want to do that?"

"No, I'd rather do all the other things we have to take up our time," Rak said. "Of course I want to go. Maybe we just need to get some eyeballs out there."

"I'll go, too," Bria said.

Mik looked to Zia. "Want to make it a party, Zia?"

"Like I said, I'm happy here."

"Fair enough," Mik said, turning to Rak and Bria. "We're at an all-stop. Suit up and hop out."

Mik and Zia waited in silence, watching the flashing beacon while the other two put on their space suits and stepped into the void. Soon Bria and Rak floated into view, their thrusters puffing them along as they moved in front of the ship.

"We getting close?" Rak asked.

Mik pressed the intercom button. "Slow up a little bit. You're about three yards away. Move up a yard."

The two spacewalkers adjusted for the instruction.

"Slower," Mik said. "Slow . . . now stop."

They angled their thrusters to stop their momentum. Then they floated, face-to-face, circling the emptiness where the signal came from.

"Now what?" Bria asked.

"Now you're facing whatever's sending the signal," Mik said.

"There's nothing here," Rak said. *"I'm going to use magnification."*

"Great idea," Zia said.

They waited while Rak made the adjustments.

"Still nothing. Increasing magnification."

Mik sighed heavily. Zia looked at him, sorry for his disappointment, but glad it was likely a scanning glitch.

"Might be best to run a thorough diagnostic on the sensors, Mik," Bria said.

"Hold it! I've got something!" Rak said.

Zia and Mik sat up straight, breathless.

"It's very small," Rak said.

"What is it?" Mik asked.

"Some kind of crystal. Tiny. Like a grain of sand."

"That's sending the signal?" Zia asked.

"Is there anything else out there?" Mik asked. "Anything at all?"

"No. Nothing."

"Could something that small send a signal that powerful?" Zia asked.

"What else it could be?" Mik said.

He turned to the console.

"Now that we talk about it, the signal has stopped," he said.

"It wanted to be found, and now it's been found," Bria said.

"Is that good news or bad?" Zia asked.

"It's your ship, Mik," Rak said. *"Should I bring it aboard?"*

Mik didn't hesitate. "Yes. Bring it in. Just run it through decontamination."

Mik and Zia paced outside the air lock as they waited for the other two. When Rak and Bria entered the air lock, the other two watched through the window as Bria put the crystal through a decontamination scan.

"That only looks for known contaminates," Zia said.

"Best we can do," Mik said.

The scan only took seconds. Rak gave Mik a thumbs-up, and Mik opened the air lock. Rak handed Mik a small, transparent pouch.

"Behold, our great discovery," Rak said.

They took it to the lab. Mik used the smallest pair of lab tweezers to put the crystal under a microscope that broadcast its magnified image on a wall monitor.

The amber-colored crystal was a translucent, asymmetrical bunch of angles and sharp edges.

"Yeah, just a grain of sand," Bria said.

"Space dust," Rak said.

"Looks like sand or maybe a crystal," Zia said. "Scans can't identify the substance, though. No telling what it is or where it came from."

"Other than the signal, big whoop," Mik said.

"That's a mighty big 'other than,'" Zia said.

"Yes, it is," Mik said.

Mik shined a bright beam of light on the crystal. The light penetrated the gem.

"Nothing inside," Zia said. "No tiny mechanism to generate a signal. This doesn't make any sense."

"The answer is obvious," Rak said. "The signal came from some-where or something else."

"Then why did the signal stop when we found the crystal?" Bria asked.

"Coincidence," Rak said.

Bria rolled her eyes.

"Okay, then. The signal came from a grain of sand. Much more believable," Rak said. "I'm going back to sleep. Please wake me when it's my watch."

They watched him leave.

"I guess I can't argue with him," Bria said. "It's not doing anything. I guess I'll go back to sleep, too."

Mik and Zia were alone.

"What do you think?" Mik asked.

Zia stared at the monitor. "Kind of a let-down."

"I suppose so. All we can do is wait, I guess. Want to go back to sleep? We can reset the watch schedule. I'll take the first one."

"Okay."

Zia left as Mik carefully put the crystal in the smallest lidded container in the lab. Then he secured the container in a locked cabinet. He laughed to himself, taking such precautions with what appeared to be a grain of sand, but he wasn't ready to let go of the sense of importance it gave him.

He returned to the cockpit and settled into the pilot's seat as time passed slowly on his watch. The steady hum of the engines failed to lull him as it did the others. He could only think of home. He heard the screams of the dying and clenched his eyes shut. The wails of the damned continued without mercy. Mik's eyes popped open.

The screams were not in his imagination. Inside his head, yes, but coming from without, somehow. Present in his mind, yet sounding as if they came from far away.

He stood and looked around the cockpit, down the corridor leading to the other areas of the ship. The atmosphere felt heavy and sinister. The stillness had lost its comforting effect. Something had changed. But what?

The crystal. That was what.

In the lab, he found the other three waiting. They had the crystal back on the lab table, projected onto the monitor. All three of them leaned into close to the crystal. Listening.

"You heard it, too?" Mik asked.

They jumped in surprise, cursing him for not making noise when he walked.

"You mean screaming? Yes." Bria said.

"This is no mere grain of sand," Rak said, turning to Bria. "You were right."

"Not sure I take pleasure in being right," Bria said.

"Obviously this thing has capabilities we can sense but don't understand," Mik said. "So the question is, what do we do here?"

"You mean get rid of it?" Zia asked.

"Or try to understand it," Mik said. "It's my ship, but I want this to be a group decision. We're in the middle of nowhere. With no home. No destination. If this is some kind of miracle substance, it might help if we can get back home."

"Back home?" Bria asked. "We're a year's travel away from the stargate."

"At least it's an option," Mik said.

"If it's a beacon, it might lead us somewhere," Rak said.

"Or lead someone to us," Bria said. "Which could be good or all kinds of bad."

"The unknown is part of life now," Zia said.

"Let's try to crack it," Bria said. "I can't stand being on this tiny ship for the rest of my life. No offense, Mik. I'm grateful for your rescue, but I'm not living like this much longer. If this thing means a new home, fine. If it kills me. Also fine."

A hush fell over the room as they processed Bria's seeming indifference to death.

"I'm for examining it, too," Mik said. "Rak? Zia?"

"Let's check it out," Rak said. "I'm bored, so let's liven things up."

Everyone looked to Zia.

"I say put it back into space," she said. "If it's not already too late."

They tried to hide their disappointment.

"What we went through to get away from that attack. The things I saw, heard . . . smelled. All I want is to forget. I like the peace and quiet. You all want to get away from it. I want to just wrap up in it and breathe. Just forget. That's all I want. This little crystal is only going to make me remember, keep my mind moving. I'm sorry, I know you wanted a unanimous vote. It's okay. I'm outnumbered. Do what you want to do, but leave me out of it. I can watch the conn while you work on it."

She turned from the lab, paused at the doorway.

"Just remember it was screams we heard," she said. "If it were angels singing, that might be something, although we don't know what kind of deceptions might be at play. Whatever you find, be careful."

They looked at each other as Zia stopped at the doorway again.

"Can you still hear them? The screams?" she asked.

The others nodded yes.

"Funny. They've gone quiet for me."

She left the lab.

Rak shook his head in irritation. "She was always dramatic. Best she keeps her distance, anyway."

"Let's focus on how this thing is communicating with us," Bria said.

"No transmitting mechanism inside of it," Rak said. "Unless it is really, really tiny."

"Could be the substance of the crystal is the mechanism," Mik said. "Remember, it's composition is a mystery."

"It sent a signal that our sensors picked up," Rak said. "We didn't hear that in our minds, so it sends different types of signals."

"I think we can go with the substance being the mechanism," Bria said.

"So we're back to our original question," Mik said. "How?"

"The sounds were internal," Rak said. "It wasn't vibrations traveling through the air to our ears. It was internal. Of that I'm certain."

"I agree," Mik said.

"Communication by mind," Bria said. "Telepathy?"

"Psychic crystal?" Rak asked.

"We have to put aside any preconceived notions," Bria said. "This crystal could be anything from sand of an alien beach to a living god of an unknown universe."

"A living god that communicates with screaming?" Rak asked.

"Why not?" Mik said.

"Okay then," Rak said. "It sent thoughts to us. We send them back."

"How? We don't know their language," Mik said.

"With images then," Bria said. "It's sensory. It can send sounds. Safe to assume it can send and receive images."

Rak nodded. "Not a bad idea. Assuming they have eyes and see like we do."

"You're getting the hang of this," Mik said.

"They have to process images at least kind of like we do," Rak said.

"There must be some universal symbols they understand. Otherwise, we may as well join Zia."

"We don't want to send jumbled messages," Bria said. "So I'll conjure the images in my mind. I'll tell you both what I'm picturing so you can think it, too. Then we'll be unified."

"Good idea," Mik said.

Rak looked around. "So, how do we go about this?"

Bria reached out to hold hands with Rak and Mik, who stood on either side of her.

"Let's hold hands," she said. "That should unify us. We'll reach out with our minds and see if we get a response."

They held hands.

"Close your eyes," she said. "No matter what happens. Keep them closed until I say."

Hands held, eyes closed, they listened to their breathing against the soft hum of the engines.

"I'm the only one who speaks from now on," she said.

No one argued.

"Darkness."

She waited for them to set darkness in their minds.

". . . A growing light. The sun being born . . ."

". . . A human being. Bria . . ."

". . . A human being. Mik . . ."

". . . A human being. Rak . . ."

". . . Alone . . ."

". . . Lost . . ."

I see you. I hear you.

Everyone jumped and clenched each other's hands, but they kept focus. The voice that entered their minds was very low and masculine, but calm

"Who are you?" Bria asked.

I am the Lord of Hanngee.

"Where is Hanngee?"

Within the crystal.

"Is Hanngee a place we can go?"

Most certainly.

"Is it a nice place? We heard screaming."

The crystal contains the history of our people. It was not always pleasant.

"How are things now?"

There is order. You are most welcome to join us.

They sat in silence, worried that speaking aloud might break the connection.

Of course, you could continue on your journey.

"Are there planets or space stations nearby?"

I'm afraid I do not know. I am the Lord of Hanngee. I have little knowledge of the outer realms, and can make no guarantees.

"What kind of place is Hanngee?"

A place of wonders. A place of fulfillment and care. Free of want. I have such sights to show you all.

"Can we talk about this amongst ourselves?"

Please do. Just know that the crystal abides in space. You must pass through the Gate of Hanngee, or set the crystal back into the void. To leave it on your ship will bring its destruction. The Gate will soon close. I await your decision.

They opened their eyes.

"I'll be damned," Mik said. "It's an alien world. In that little crystal."

"Talk about expanding your mind," Rak said.

"Sounds like utopia," Bria said.

"The only utopias I know of are false," Mik said.

"So you're staying with the ship?" Rak asked.

"I didn't say that. What about you?"

"Oh, I'm going," Rak said. "If it means death, at least it's an adventure. Better than wasting away on this crate. No offense."

"I'm going, too," Bria said. "I'm certain it means death. I'm ready."

The men looked at Bria for a second.

"I could be wrong," she said. "Just a feeling."

"I think you're crazy," Rak said. "We've discovered another world.

Why wouldn't we run through its gates?"

"Lord of Hanngee," Bria said.

I am still here.

"Are we, men and women of flesh and blood, able to live in your realm?"

You are. The Gate of Hanngee prepares all who pass through.

"My Lord," Mik said. "Can you offer passage to Hanngee to the people of our world?"

It would be my pleasure. Indeed, many of your people are already here. Mila and Equi.

"My parents!" Bria said.

The gate will close momentarily.

"I'm going," Rak said.

"Me, too," Mik said.

Bria ran from the room to the cockpit. She breathlessly told a wide-eyed Zia about all that had happened.

"We're going," Bria said when the tale was told. "What about you? Want to come?"

"No. I'll stay here."

"How can you stay here! This is an empty void. Absolutely nothing for millions of miles."

"So be it. This is where my story ends. I don't trust the crystal."

Mik and Rak came into the cockpit.

"We'll miss you, Zia," Mik said.

"Fair winds and calm seas," Rak said.

Zia stood to hug her companions.

"How will this all work?" Zia asked.

"I guess we'll find out," Rak said with a grin.

"Best wishes to all of you," Zia said. "Goodbye."

She returned to the cockpit seat. The others looked at each other as if to confirm their commitment, then returned to the lab.

"This is it!" Rak said.

"Tell him we're ready, Bria," Mik said.

They stood in a circle and joined hands.

"We are ready, Lord of Hanngee."

The tiny crystal pulsed with red light. In seconds, crimson lightning stabbed into the room, reaching out to the trio with jagged tendrils of light. They clenched in apprehension.

"It tickles," Bria said with a giggle.

"Warm, too," Rak said.

The lightning intensified. The crystal expanded, slowly growing from cup size to table size and then rapidly widening.

Zia bolted upright in her chair at the sounds of screaming. Something had gone wrong.

She stood and looked down the hallway. A bright red light flashed from the lab, reflecting off the hallway walls. The screams were the familiar voices of her shipmates. Zia put her hands on her head, stressing, tears pouring from her eyes.

"Mik! Bria! Rak!"

The screams grew louder as the light traveled down the hallway toward her. A wall of red, pulsating glow emerged from metal walls of the corridor, like an expanding bubble bringing a new dimension within. Zia backed up and hit the cockpit chair. There was nowhere to go. She screamed and covered her eyes.

A ripple of electricity shook her body as the wall of the red bubble passed through her, leaving her standing in a new world, a new reality.

She stood before a massive, wrought-iron gate. It reached as high into the clouds of this strange world, as did the stone walls, which stretched out endlessly to the left and right. The dirt she stood on, the sky and the clouds, all were red, as was the giant figure standing before her. He was twice as tall as Mik or Rak, who struggled against the grasp of a horde of bug-like beings, as did Bria. All three of them thrashed and screamed in terror, begging Zia to help them.

I am the Lord of Hanngee, Zia. You have wisely chosen the endless void of space.

Zia shook with fear at the large being. His skin was red like his cloak. Two thick horns spiraled out of his bald scalp. His face was friendly, but his eyes were without mercy.

Mik and the others continued to scream themselves hoarse with mindless fear. The towering gate squealed open, and a squadron of bug-like creatures streamed out to pull her friends into what lie beyond. When the gates opened, the screams and wails of torment from perhaps millions of doomed souls assaulted her ears.

"Can they be saved?" Zia asked the Lord of Hanngee. "Set them free, please!"

I am the receiver of souls. The conqueror of all worlds. Behold . . .

He stood aside and beckoned Zia to peek through the gates. Certain she had no choice, she stepped to the gate and looked through.

The land beyond the gate was ringed by jagged red mountains. Although there was a round, red sun, the land was cloaked in a suffocating gloom. In the central valley, she saw masses of people crying out for relief from the dismemberment and bloodshed of the bug-like beings. Past the mountain peaks, she saw an array of planets in the red sky.

Yes, Zia. I take the souls. I take entire worlds for my pleasure. It is I who created the void in which you will finish your days in loneliness.

The far wall of the red bubble approached in the distance, coming toward them, as the sphere of this alternate reality passed by and moved on.

Rest well, Zia.

The creatures wrestled Zia's companions through the gate, screaming and crying as they reached for her in vain. There was nothing she could do. The Lord of Hanngee smiled and bid farewell with a polite nod. He stepped through the gates as the opposite bubble wall passed, leaving Zia back in the ship's cockpit.

Stunned and feeling drunk, she turned to look out the cockpit window.

The red bubble had shrunk down to the size of a plate. It continued to contract until it could no longer be seen.

Zia collapsed into the cockpit chair. She focused on the rumble of the engines in order to drown out the echoes of their screams.

Gamorra Apple Jam

The road on which I drove, so straight for most of my long journey, turned winding and jagged, along with my thoughts. The main turn-pike, cut through the flattest land available to aid in quick travel, was almost dangerously dull, urging me toward an untimely sleep. I fol-lowed my handwritten directions and left the parade of minivans and semi-trucks. I struck north, alone on a desolate highway.

I stopped at a small town along the way to relieve myself, refuel, and grab a refreshment. While I paid for my soda and gas, the kind lady behind the register inquired of my well-being and destination in the easy way such folk seem to do. I told her I was bound for Gamorra Fields, and would she mind verifying my directions? She reacted as if I were Jonathan Harker asking directions to the Borgo Pass. She took a cursory glance at my paper and nodded. Yes, that would get me there.

She recovered her good humor just as I was about to ask what had so upset her about the mention of Gamorra Fields. Can't have you leave on an empty stomach, she said. She summoned her bag boy and had him fill a bag with lunch from the tiny deli. I paused in silence, not knowing how to react.

While he left to run his errand, she asked if I was passing through or staying. I told her I was staying. She asked me now long I intended to stay. Taken aback by her sudden concern, I stuttered a little as I told her I had no idea for sure, but planned to stay the weekend at the long-est. She seemed mostly relieved at this and warned me about the blind curves and occasional fog I was certain to encounter. Best to slow down and be safe. Be safe, she repeated.

Her demeanor amped up considerably from her initial friendliness. It was as if someone had lowered the knob controlling her mood at the mention of Gamorra Fields and had now turned it way up past its regular setting.

The bag boy returned with my lunch. Not wanting any further weirdness, I took out my wallet to pay for the extra items I hadn't asked for. The lady waved me off. This one's on me, she said, and if you're sensible, you'll buy some groceries here for the weekend. Best to have the larders stocked so you don't have to eat out for all of your meals. She even offered me a discount on my total bill.

Ready to get out of there, I politely declined and thanked her for the free lunch. She stood at the door as I walked to my car.

"Best not to give in to temptation," she said.

I considered a witty rejoinder, but held back at the expression on her face.

"May the Lord be with you, Sir," she said.

When I turned back, she had entered the store. The glass door eased shut behind her.

I shook my head and got into the car. The lunch bag contained a sandwich of ham salad on rye bread, a bag of chips, and a liter of Coke. My mouth watered.

I looked to the store to wave my final thanks, but she wasn't looking. I could see her though. She had joined hands with the bag boy. Their eyes were closed. Heads bowed. Lips moving. Praying.

Easy, then, to deduce that Gamorra Fields was not a favored place here. Could be for any reason, perhaps a football rivalry. Who knew what kind of people the store lady and the bag boy were? Even the kindest people could be completely off their nut. I didn't know these people, nor the people of Gamorra Fields, so I considered it a waste of time to pick a side. I readied my ham salad sandwich, took a delicious bite, and drove on.

A distant relative—a great-grand uncle I'd never met—had bequeathed me a house in Gamorra Fields. The house along with everything in it. I received a certified letter from his attorney informing me of the inheritance. It took great effort to find the closest living kin to my great-grand uncle, Alastor McKibben. That relative was me. I remembered that idle Tuesday morning had begun with work on a magazine article at home. By lunchtime, I owned a house three states away in a village I'd never heard of.

There was a curious twist to this notification—the attorney included with the inheritance an offer to buy the house on the spot. The money he offered was generous. I had no mortgage, and this was basically a gift of free money. I gave serious thought to selling the house, collecting my check, and moving up to a higher standard of living.

I hesitated, though. There was only the enclosed photo to know what the house looked like—an old, Gothic Victorian. Dark gray with black trim. The offered price matched the home seen in the photo. The responsible thing to do was spend the time and expense to travel to Gamorra Fields and do a visual inspection. Maybe the house was worth more. Offering it on the open market might drive up the price. Gamorra Fields might be a nice, quiet place to live and write. Or even a weekend getaway. I had no family. I had nothing but options. So I contacted the attorney, thanked him for the offer, but told him I wanted to see the house in person before making any decisions. He asked when I would come and told me—in glorious small-town fashion—that the key would be in the mailbox when I arrived.

I wrapped up my freelance writing obligations and cleared a few days for a trip to Gamorra Fields. Internet research showed images of a nice, bucolic village out of a Hawthorne novel. An isolated tiny hamlet nestled away from the world in the hills and woods. Only a few hundred people. "Only" a few hundred years old. The local economy depended on agriculture, mostly fruit trees. Nothing seemed out of the ordinary, unless cleanliness and quiet is unusual in this day and age.

It wasn't until my encounter at the roadside diner/gas station that I felt any sense of unease. The turnpike was far behind me, along with the wide, level landscape. Now I encountered the treacherous curves the lady warned me about. Steep hills forced me to drop my car into a lower gear. Thick banks of fog hugged the road. More than once I had to creep along at the speed of a slow walk, praying a truck wouldn't come roaring into me. Sometimes, I had stretches where I had to deal with fog, a steep incline, and a curve. All at once.

Finally I broke clear of fog. The curves straightened out. The sharp upgrades settled into rolling, pleasant hills. I entered a wide forest. The canopy of foliage overhead was so thick I had to turn on my headlights. The dark woods, along with the strange behavior of the gas station lady, set my mind running riot. I imagined all sorts of creepy scenarios I might encounter, inspired by the movies, films, and books I consumed against the admonitions of my parents, who seemed very wise in that moment.

I passed a clearing in the woods centered by an old house. Then another. Gradually, the scattered houses coalesced into town streets and neighborhoods. I passed a building that looked like a church. It had no steeple, so perhaps it had been repurposed.

A single stoplight crowned main street. The center avenue held a grocery store, a laundry, a bank, and other essential businesses for a small town. A couple of cars and a pickup were parked in front of the grocery store. It was there I parked to consult the town map sent by the attorney.

It was so close I could have walked. I drove anyway. The old Victorian dominated its block. It was visible as soon as I turned onto the street. The driveway was clean and level under the wheels of my car. I got out and stretched, taking in the impressive sight of my Uncle Alastor's house. My house now.

Neat paint covered the house and trim. The lawn was green, lush, and free of weeds. The hedges were clipped nice and tight. It was a corner lot. I studied the large windows. The turret rose higher than I expected and no doubt had a magnificent view. Even without seeing the inside, even though it was in a small town, I had no doubt I could get a much higher price than the attorney had offered.

The key was in the mailbox by the front door as promised. The deadbolt threw back with a quick, clean click. I stepped into my ancestor's home and back in time.

Everything was dark, polished wood. Dusted and clean. Gorgeous woven rugs covered the floors. Antique furniture graced its rooms. The ceilings were high and bore glittering chandeliers. Thick curtains flanked the picture windows. I walked through a dining hall, a parlor, a TV room, and a large kitchen. I smiled as the stairs creaked under my shoes. There were three large bedrooms upstairs, all furnished. I entered the turret and found the den. Full bookshelves circled the round room, floor to ceiling. A grand oak desk sat at the center of the room, facing the window, that—confirming my guess—faced the surrounding woods. This would be a heavenly place to work. I knew then I would never sell this house. I had already named it—McKibben Manor.

I came downstairs to someone calling hello. A slight, dignified older man stood in the foyer.

"Hope I'm not intruding," he said.

He had prominent brown eyes behind wire-rimmed glasses. His suit was well-fitted to his thin frame. A lawyer out of central casting. We shook hands.

"Not at all," I said. "Mr. Philip, I presume."

"Guilty as charged," he said. "I'm glad you found the place. You had a pleasant trip, I hope?"

"A long drive, but very scenic."

"Good to hear. Say, sorry to jump right to business, but have you considered my offer to purchase?"

No more small talk, then.

"Considering it, but leaning towards no," I said.

His smile downshifted to more of a teeth-baring expression.

"No? Shame. Well, everything's a negotiation as they say in my business," he said. "Would you like to hear a counteroffer?"

"I'm not the kind of man who likes to rush things, Mr. Philip," I said. "If it's all the same, I'd like to take the weekend to stay in the house, see how it fits."

The teeth were gone. "You're planning to move here?"

"No law against that, right?"

"Certainly not, but would this be the best place for a freelance writer to base his operations?"

He saw the look on my face.

"I'm sorry," he said. "I learned of your profession while tracking you down. All on the up-and-up, I assure you."

"Fair enough. But on the contrary, a secluded place of peace and quiet is just what a writer looks for," I said. "However, the money you are offering would allow me to buy a nice home just about anywhere. But I also have family history and tradition to consider. I didn't even know my great-grand uncle. Lots of writing fodder there, you see?"

"I do indeed," he said, softening. "Do you have family?"

"Just me."

"You have extended family still with you?"

"Only child. Parents are passed."

"I'm very sorry."

"So as you can see, it's just me."

He nodded, appearing to think hard on something, then took a deep breath, as if he'd made a decision. I assumed he had surrendered to my decision to put off the choice of buying or selling.

"Well, if you're going to be with us for the weekend, to 'check us out' so to speak, you'll have to try the local specialty," he said.

He led me into the spacious kitchen, opening various cupboard doors, looking for something. I felt a pang of sorrow at seeing such detail of the recent life of my ancestor. I regretted never knowing him, a man of my own blood.

Mr. Philip's search revealed plates and cups, boxes of seasonings and stove-top dinners, several cans of Spam.

"Ah! Here we go!" he said.

He turned to face me, brandishing a jar of jam.

"Gamorra Apple Jam!" he said with a big, proud smile. "Best jam you can buy. Delicious! And addictive. Our market share is small, but our distribution is worldwide."

I had never heard of it. "It's made here?"

"Oh yes! We grow and pick the apples. They grow here and nowhere else in the world. We make the jam and can it."

I examined the jar, twisted off the lid and looked at the dark crimson spread.

"Why do you color it red?" I asked.

"Oh, we don't. That's its natural color."

He dug around some more and found a loaf of bread. "You simply must try it."

Just like that, the aroma of cooking toast filled the room as he dropped the bread in the old appliance. He fished through the silverware drawer for a butter knife. I found this all pretty weird, but he was a hometown boy proud of the hometown specialty.

That toast aroma had an odd effect. Maybe it was the hearty ham sandwich I had eaten on the drive up, but I wasn't remotely hungry. Indeed, the thought of eating anything made me queasy. I grimaced and told him I was stuffed after a road meal and that it would be much better if I tried it when I had the appetite.

He gave me a blank stare for about two seconds, then shrugged, and took the toast as it popped up.

"Do you mind?" he asked as he began spreading jam over the toast.

They sure do like their jam, I thought. I listened to him crunch away while I ducked into the dining hall to look around.

The intricately carved chairs sat regally around the long dining table. I wondered which chair my uncle preferred to sit at. Did he eat alone? Host lively dinner parties? In the corner was a hutch containing all manner of fascinating knick-knacks from what I assumed was worldwide travel. The more I explored the house, the more I needed to know who Alastor McKibben was. It also became more unlikely I would sell the house. I'm a loner by nature. If the village of Gamorra Fields rejected me, so be it. I would lose no sleep over it.

Mr. Philip joined me in the dining room, cleaning his mouth with a napkin. The red jam left blood-like spots on his lips and teeth. I didn't know whether to laugh or start running.

"Forgive me," he said, chuckling. "I hadn't had my lunch yet. You'll understand when you try this jam."

He watched me, probably divining my growing affection for the house.

"It's a busy weekend for us," he said. "We have the apple harvest this weekend. Starting at sunup tomorrow morning. The whole village pitches in. After the apples are brought in, there will be a church service and then a party in the village square. Would you like to take part? It's quite a shindig."

I didn't care for the "sunup" part of the deal, but I was a writer eternally on the lookout for an interesting story, and there was no denying my life had taken an incredible turn.

"If you'd rather keep to yourself, we understand," he said. "We're the keep-to-ourselves kind as well."

"Yes, I think I'd like to join you."

He brightened. "Excellent! Like I said, it's at sunup. Just leave your bedroom curtains open, and the morning light will wake you when it's time. We'll gather on main street. There'll be trucks to take us to the tree. Do you have work clothes with you?"

"Not really."

"Hardware store on Main will fix you up. It'll be cold throughout the day, so keep that in mind. Each worker gets a basket of apples for payment. When you taste them, you'll know it's better than getting paid with money!"

"Looking forward to it," I said. Then something struck me. "I'm sorry, did you say we'll get a ride to 'the tree?' Singular?"

He laughed. "You'll see tomorrow. Another source of local pride."

He put his hands in his pockets and rocked up on the balls of his feet, all chipper and happy. I relaxed, feeling like I'd been accepted a little. He bid me farewell and left.

Agreeing to the harvest was a smart move. He would likely put in a good word for me around town. No matter my ultimate decision, I wanted to make a good impression on the people of the village.

I spent a few hours exploring the house. My hope was to find any of Alastor's personal effects—photo albums, documents, maybe a dairy, but there was nothing. I made a mental note to press Mr. Philip about whether such things had been removed. His expression would give me my answer, no matter what his words. I stretched out on the spare room bed and drifted off for a short nap.

My appetite woke me up at dusk. I took a stroll down to the hardware store for some work clothes, then walked next door to the local restaurant for dinner. I was in the mood for some old-fashioned American chow, so I had the double cheeseburger. It was gourmet and much better than I anticipated. The Gamorra apple was ubiquitous. It was available not only as jam for bread, but drinkable in a cider, a glaze for the spare ribs, and more. I'm the kind of guy who stiffens up under pressure, so I declined their repeated suggestions to make the jam any part of my meal. Maybe at the festival I would make a show of trying it to see if it lived up to its reputation.

I ate alone and kept to myself. The other villagers didn't stare, but their self-conscious non-staring was even more uncomfortable. All of them made jam part of their meal, of course. I tried not to notice, but the red substance staining everyone's mouth made me force down a giggle. The little children looked like vampires with the stuff all over their mouths.

It was a dark walk home. The utter quiet was something new. I looked up to see stars I had never seen. On balance, I decided small-town life as something I could get accustomed to.

The curtains were still open, which made me uncomfortable. I drew them all shut and also made sure the doors were locked, curious if living in this village would purge me of that big-city habit.

The jar of apple jam was still on the counter. I was tempted to scoop out a spoonful and get it over with, but once again, a full belly kept the temptation at bay.

Sleeping in my uncle's bed was an unsettling proposition. However, it was my house and bed now, and I would have to sleep in it sooner or later. Unsure if the bedding had been changed (also wondering if this was where he had died, I needed to collect some details), I found spare sheets in the linen closet and changed them out. After that busy work and a heavy meal, I was ready for sleep. It came quickly.

Sunup stirred me awake as promised. I stretched and looked out my bedroom window. A stream of humanity flowed through the streets, heading for Main Street. I quickly dressed in my new clothes, which consisted of work jeans and a flannel shirt. I jogged downstairs and out the door to join everyone else. People were all smiles and waves, much friendlier than before. My decision to help out with the harvest had gained me a measure of acceptance as I'd hoped.

On Main Street I found a fleet of flatbed trucks idling in a row. A couple of trucks were loaded with stacks of large wicker baskets and ladders. Workers jumped up and crowded onto the other trucks for a ride. I followed my line of people and hopped up onto the nearest one. I looked around and spotted Mr. Philip, who waved and smiled from the next truck. I had to admit I was caught up in the local excitement and was ready to get to work.

A ten-minute drive took the convoy out of the village and into the woods. The road was rough, and we laughed as we tried to keep our spots as the truck rumbled and bounced through the rough terrain. After a slight incline we came upon a wide pasture dominated by a tree so big and expansive I first thought it was a series of trees on a large hill.

The trunk was as wide as a building. Its roots, the size of an average tree, sprouted off from the trunk and sprawled out, tapering off and descending into the ground like spindly spider legs. The branches reached up and out, forming a huge canopy of thick green leaves. A magnificent, mountainous tree, unlike any I had ever seen.

As the trucks wound closer to the tree, I studied the ground as we passed and did a double-take. Gravestones filled the pasture, rows upon rows of them. Their position was odd. Every marker faced the tree like rows of soldiers from a vast army.

I watched everyone gaze at the tree with reverent awe. Although the trucks followed winding dirt roads through the sprawling cemetery, I still felt uneasy rumbling through the final resting place of what had to be hundreds, if not thousands, of people. My companions didn't appear to think it odd or disrespectful.

The trucks stopped around the tree. Everyone dove out and got to work, all coordinated like worker ants. Mr. Philip found me and brought me over to his small group. Together with a group of men and women, we found an unoccupied spot along the trunk with a ladder and baskets. The smell of diesel fumes wafted away on the fall wind, replaced by the cinnamon-tinged aroma of fresh, ripe apples.

The youngsters energetically set about collecting the fruit that had fallen to the ground.

"Any qualms about climbing the tree, Mr. McKibben?" Mr. Philip asked.

I felt like a little boy at the prospect of ascending such a grand tree. While my companions placed and adjusted the ladder, I felt the bark of the tree, appreciating its sturdiness. The bark was unlike any I'd felt before. It wasn't as rough, but had a soft, almost rubbery feel to it, and —unless my senses deceived me—a touch of comforting warmth.

One of my companions slung the straps of ten empty burlap bags over my shoulder.

"Ready, Mr. McKibben?"

I nodded and climbed the ladder. It took me up to the main crook of the ancient trunk.

"Just climb on up as high as you can," Mr. Philip said. "Well, as high as you're comfortable, I mean."

The branches were thick and sturdy, so I climbed and stopped just before the branches bowed further under my weight than was safe. I estimate I was forty feet in the air. Mr. Philip and the others climbed up behind me, stationed downward so we could each reach down to the other. It was straightforward, as Mr. Philip explained. Just fill a bag with apples and pass it down when full, then start filling another bag. He would guide me as to how far to the right and left to go, then we would work our way down.

I got my first good look at the Gamorra apples. They were the color of red velvet, even having a slight, furry velvety feel. Shaped more like a pear than an apple, it was twice as large as either fruit. I grabbed the apple and gave it a twist. It snapped free from the branch. For a moment, I considered how unusual it was.

"I've never seen anything like this," I said.

Mr. Philip stood on a lower branch smiling at me, patient. "They don't grow anywhere else in the world."

"Only here? On this one tree?" I asked.

He smiled and nodded, amused at my reaction.

A tree this size was worth a moderately sized orchard of "normal" trees. I was sure to get one hell of a story out of this.

I shrugged and placed the apple into my bag. My work day had begun. Other workers picked nearby and in the distance. We passed down the bags until they reached the workers on the ground, who carefully placed them in the wicker baskets and loaded them onto the flatbeds. When the flatbeds were full, they would drive off and return later, empty.

After a lunch break, we switched positions. I returned to the ground where two female companions showed me the proper way to pack the apples in the baskets. During a lull in the picking, one of them took an apple and snatched a hearty bite. The juice ran down her chin, and its bloody color startled me for a second. She looked like a vampire, and I said so. She looked at her companion, and they giggled. She offered me a bite, but I declined. Still wasn't the time. Mr. Philip was right, though. There was no need to use artificial coloring in the jam.

The day passed quickly. The work was hard and sweaty, but the company was enjoyable. The air was crisp and cool. The sun rolled overhead. By the time we'd stripped the tree of that year's fruit and the workers relaxed to catch their breath, the sun was fat and low behind the treetops.

I sat on a flatbed as they placed the last of the baskets upon it. Mr. Philip walked up to the truck.

"I think we're done," he said. "One of our biggest harvests. What do you think?"

"I enjoyed it," I said. "But I have to ask you something, if you don't mind."

"Anything."

"Why do all of these graves face the tree?"

He took the question in stride. "The tree provides our livelihood. We have a truly unique relationship with it. We remember it at the end of our days."

I nodded, hiding my discomfort. Although not an overly religious man myself, the funerals I had attended commended the souls of the dead to God, not a tree.

The work was done. Everyone gathered around the tree, facing toward it from all directions, just like the gravestones. A tall man with white hair stepped forward, face-to-face with the wide trunk. He spread his open hands at his sides, and the others did so as well. He closed their eyes. So did they. I remained still, uncomfortable taking part, but glad everyone had their eyes closed.

"Almighty Gamorra," the white-haired man said. "We thank thee for another bountiful harvest. We beseech thee to maintain your protective hand over our hamlet you established so long ago. Give us everlasting courage to do what must be done. We are your faithful servants."

"*Almighty Gamorra,*" the crowd chanted.

Their eyes opened, and everyone came out of their reverence with a sense of joy and celebration. There was laughter and backslapping and we boarded the flatbed trucks for the return trip to the village.

"Next we'll gather for church," Mr. Philip informed me. "You can freshen up at your new home. We'll gather at six p.m."

I stood under a hot shower, washing away the dirt and sweat of the day, letting the steam clear my head from a satisfying day's work. The weather beautiful. Still, there was an unsettling sense of . . . I wasn't sure what. Difficult to know if my unease was that of an outsider among insiders, or an instinctual warning of danger. I reconsidered my decision to stay and keep the house, but decided to ride out the weekend, perhaps stay for another week and experience the village in normal circumstances before passing final judgment upon it. How would an alien react, I thought, if it were to land on Earth in the middle of Halloween festivities?

I dried and dressed and sat in the dark den for a few moments, feeling comfortable for the first time since I arrived. I reckoned my preference for solitude had me out of sorts. I rocked back and forth in the old office chair, listening to it creak. How much weirdness could be chalked up to small-town idiosyncrasies and isolation? Was the use of the word "weirdness" unfair? I didn't think so. The tree was weird, as was its fruit, the texture of its bark, and the pagan-like devotion on the part of the villagers, who regarded the tree as a deity, even dedicating their dead to it. What would happen if I declared my agnosticism to it all? Refused to be a regular participant in the yearly revel? What would they make of that? What would they do?

The peal of the church bell brought me out of my escalating paranoia. I stood at the turret window and saw streams of people on the move again, this time toward the church with no cross. Wanting to join the group before Mr. Philip felt compelled to come looking for me, I went outside, pulling on my jacket.

A pang of nostalgia swept through me as I entered the church. There was plenty to remind me of the old country churches of my youth. Small scratches marred the polished old wood pews. The ancient carpet sent a slight mildew smell into the air. People in their Sunday best laughed and hobnobbed as they filed in.

There were differences from those churches I remembered. No crosses. No paintings of Jesus. No felt banners with embroidered Bible verses. Plenty of plants and small trees about though.

An organist played a particularly grim-sounding dirge. I frowned at the first sign of melancholy since I arrived.

"What do you think of our little church, Mr. McKibben?"

Mr. Philip had appeared at my side again, hands in pockets, rolling up and down on his feet.

"Very nice," I said. "Although the music is a bit more dire than I expected. You know, after the festive mood I've encountered all day."

He had a solemn look. "It's meant to remind us of Gamorra's terrible power. That it is only through her mercy—and our obedience—that we survive year to year."

After giving me a look to make sure I understood the gravity of his point, he left to find a seat.

I knew then that there was not even a pretense of Christian tradition in Gamorra Fields. Gamorra was obviously the patron deity of the village. Mr. Philip referred to Gamorra in the feminine sense. While not much of a practicing Christian, I wasn't a pagan either. Here, far from the watchful eyes of greater civilization, would one be allowed to abstain from picking a side between Jehovah and Gamorra? I worried I would soon find out. Perhaps selling the house would be the wise move.

Although everyone talked merrily amongst themselves, I knew they focused at least part of their attention on me. I sat in respectful silence and looked around the sanctuary, keeping my expression neutral.

No crosses, as expected by now. No iconography. There was a modest lectern on a small dais. Behind it was an elaborately painted mural in green. It was the tree, of course. It took up the entire wall facing the congregation. The roots wound toward the floor, reaching for a mass of yellow stars that covered the lowest part of the wall. I found that odd. The roots also reached out and crept along the side walls, twisting and turning and looping around as roots do, each one ending in a human heart. Not a cute, Valentine's Day heart, but a realistic rendition of an actual heart. It was hard to keep a straight face. By now I felt real danger, but I worried running now would be like running from an excited hound.

The white-haired man took his place behind the lectern as the sanctuary went silent. He turned and raised an open hand to the mural.

"Almighty Gamorra," Whitey said.

"*Almighty Gamorra,*" the congregants repeated.

"In the ancient of days," he said. "From stars beyond stars, the seeds of Almighty Gamorra came to our ancestors, and only our ancestors. She called from the ground in which she fell to those who founded our faith. By her mercy she provides us with what we need to be her disciples. We, in our loving turn, offer sacrifice to show our gratitude and ensure her continued mercy toward us. All those who partake of the life-giving sustenance of Almighty Gamorra are bound to her, body and spirit, to await the reward of eternal fellowship with our benevolent mother."

Boy, did I ever want a rosary. Just because.

"We have carefully tended to Her, and in return she has yielded a bountiful harvest for us to enjoy and to share with the world. Our work is done for the winter, my brothers and sisters. Almighty Gamorra is pleased and has proven her gratitude by her provision. Now our seasonal rest begins.

"So go now, my friends, to the festival of Gamorra. Enjoy yourselves and revel! As we and our people have done since the time of Almighty Gamorra's arrival, we will conclude the season under the full moon with the final offering to the goddess. It will be offered by the King and Queen of the Harvest, to be crowned at midnight!"

Cheers erupted from the congregation. I jumped in fear, but quickly reclaimed myself, stood, and applauded. By tomorrow, all of this would be over, I told myself. Tomorrow I could sell the house, which meant I had to brass it out tonight. Besides, fleeing in the dark night through the winding roads seemed foolish. I had no choice but to try to have fun for appearance's sake.

I followed the crowd out of the church and we made our way to Main Street. A huge bonfire dominated the center of the street, flanked by numerous small ones that bathed the area in orange light. A country-western band picked and grinned from atop a flatbed truck. Tables lined the sidewalks where men and women got busy peeling and dicing apples. They poured bowls of apple choppings into bubbling cauldrons and stirred. The canning and production of the jam and other apple products took place by firelight. I detected the smell of cinnamon and nutmeg and other seasonings I couldn't identify. A sheriff's deputy strolled through the party, saying hello to everyone.

I relaxed a little, being out of that infernal church. Here it was easier to pretend this was just a small-town celebration like any other I had attended. My two female companions from the harvest found me. They looked beautiful by the firelight with their long blonde hair. They pulled me into the street to shimmy to the music for a couple of songs. Music and dancing made the night feel increasingly normal. I thought the weirdness might be over.

Hot, exhausted, and parched, I asked the girls to help me find the refreshment stand. I was dying for a beer. They each took a hand and pulled me toward a busy table opposite the band. I asked for a beer. The woman behind the table handed me a dark brown bottle—no label—and I took a long pull.

By the third swallow I realized I had taken my first sample of a Gamorra apple product. Some kind of hard cider. I was nervous at crossing this threshold so unexpectedly, but the drink was delicious. Crisp, sharp, and smooth. It went down fast. By the time I reached the bottom of the bottle, I felt a pleasant, though not debilitating, buzz. I wiped some spillage from my lips. My hand was blood red when I pulled it away. My anxiety came back worse than before.

For the first time that weekend, I let my guard down and had some fun. So they were pagans. So what? There were lots of religious traditions with beliefs that must seem strange to each other. I chided myself for my cloistered thinking and drank some more. In hindsight, I know the cider dulled my thoughts.

The party did not relent for hours. The cider flowed. My companions became friendlier by the minute. Through my cider-induced haze, I thought I saw people indulging in acts usually done in private. Gamorra Fields looked more and more like a fun place to be. In my slightly inebriated state, it all seemed like a raucous college party, an exhilarating break from the day-to-day mundanity of everyday life. I even entertained the thought of joining their little church. I had no religious affiliation. What did it matter to go through the motions? Lord, how the sinister brew had dulled my instincts!

Deep into the night, ol' Whitey appeared. He strolled through the celebration with a contented smile on his face. As he made his way around, people found a stopping point for whatever they were working on, whatever song was being played, whatever joke one told, whatever intimate acts one carried out. He stood in the center of the street, patiently waiting until he had everyone's attention.

"Now, my friends," he said. "The most important part of our celebration. The crowning of the king and queen of the Gamorra Apple Festival!"

The crowd roared. I joined them.

The mass of humanity parted. Two men, each pushing a two-wheeled cart, brought their loads into the firelight. The crowd grew louder. I went silent. My mind sharpened into horror.

On each cart was a bound human being. A man on one. A woman on the other. Taped and gagged. They looked college age to me. Their breathing was fast. Their eyes wide. I looked from them to the deputy. He merely watched, bored. That took away any idea of causing a disturbance on my part. I knew perfectly well that to interrupt their holy festival was to ask for death.

The white-haired man stood before each prisoner. He moved his hands and wiggled his fingers in front of their faces as he uttered some ungodly blessing. Satisfied, he nodded and turned to the crowd.

"Brothers and sisters, the king and queen!"

More cheering. I looked around, knowing my confusion would make me stand out, but this had gone to another level of horror that even the booze could not dull.

"Now they'll take the king and queen to Almighty Gamorra.'

I spun around to find Mr. Philip at my side.

"Having fun?" he asked.

I nodded, trying not to shake. "Although this latest development makes me a little nervous."

He made a face that showed how much he understood. "I can sympathize. It's easy for us locals to forget how much we've set ourselves apart from the so-called real world."

"What's going to happen to those people?" I asked.

"They'll feed the tree," he said, as if I'd asked how faucets worked.

I remembered the mural in the church. I faced the realization I'd been trying to ignore from the moment those young people were wheeled out—they would die unless someone intervened. The only person who might help was me, and I was outnumbered.

Words cluttered my mind. So many things to ask and say at once. Mr. Philip saw my struggle. He chuckled.

"It's all right, Mr. McKibben. This is our way. It was your great-grand uncle's way. It is, you might say, part of your inheritance.

"Now, the elders will escort the king and queen to their destiny. We each take an honored guest to witness."

He fixed me with a serious look.

"Will you do me the honor of being my guest?"

Not only would they die, I would have to watch. On the other hand, if only a small group was going, the odds of me helping the couple were better. I might die in the attempt, but for the first time I worried not only for my body but my soul. Resigned, I accepted, trying to act interested and excited.

He slapped me on the shoulder. "Excellent! Now, give us a hand, will you?"

I aided the other men in loading the two-wheelers onto a flatbed truck. I did my best to communicate with my eyes to the young lady that I was a friend. When the opportunity came for me to act, I hoped she'd know the score.

There were six members of their board of elders. Not all of them brought a guest. Whitey was with us. Including the driver, there were ten of them, total. Still far too many for me to handle alone. I glanced over the young man. He looked athletic. If possible, I would spring him first. With his youth, strength, and a boost of survival adrenaline, he would be a great ally.

The truck drove back to the apple tree. The fast zig-zagging among the trees and hills nearly shattered what fortitude I had left.

We entered the open field in the center of the woods. The full, unclouded moon lit the area in silver. The endless rows of gravestones cast ominous shadows on the ground. The gigantic tree was still, despite the formidable wind. I held tight to the handles of the two-wheeled cart as the girl bound to it whimpered in fear.

Somehow these two would be sacrificed to the entity represented by the tree. Or did an actual entity dwell in the tree? If so, the forces arrayed against me were mighty indeed. I glanced at the gravestones that passed by in a blur. How many were natural deaths? How many had given their lives to Gamorra against their will?

As if to answer my question, the truck sped past the sprawling tree and crested a hill behind it. My confusion deepened. I had not come this far during the harvest, so this was new. Over the hill, I saw with horror that the cemetery was at least four times as large as I thought. In the field beyond the hill stood more rows of gravestones, far too many to count or estimate. I knew this small village was hundreds of years old. How many lives had they taken? How often did they offer human sacrifice to Gamorra?

The truck turned down a slope, and those of us on the flatbed scrambled to keep our balance and prevent the victims from rolling off. We stopped along the wall of a high cliff. The elders lit up lanterns and torches that revealed a cave opening in the wall.

Together we lifted the two-wheeled carts down to the ground. My skin crawled at the bland efficiency of it all.

Whitey, holding his torch high, led the procession into the cave. Mr. Philip gestured for me to push the young lady's cart. I got the unsettling impression he wanted my hands busy and when the time came, dirty.

The cave tunnel was smooth and wide. Great care had gone into its excavation. I pushed the cart, feeling vibrations from the young lady's terror traveling through the metal handles and into my body.

The tunnel's twists and turns were dizzying, but it wasn't a maze. No false turns or dead-ends. After a few minutes, openings appeared in the walls. They were rectangular, like bunks on a ship. Inside the openings were bodies. It was hard to catch details. I had to steal quick looks by torchlight. Some bodies were more freshly dead than others. Some were skeletons, some still decomposed. They all had one thing in common—a root descending from the dirt into their chests. Right at the heart. So that's how it happened. The openings were graves.

Some of the alcoves were empty. The scattering of long-dead and newly dead made no sense. It wasn't as if the ancient dead were in the center, tapering out to the freshly dead as one traveled to the outer tunnels. Victims were sacrificed here, some there. I couldn't make heads or tails of the system, so I didn't try. All that mattered was getting out with the two young people.

The procession slowed. Whitey looked at available wall graves, no doubt trying to make sure he was in the right place according to their mysterious criteria. While this kept the men occupied, I took stock of my situation. It was close quarters, which worked to my advantage. I could keep one occupied while the others were trapped behind him. Three of the men had pistols stuffed haphazardly into their belts. I wished I'd seen that earlier. Disarming one of them would be easy. Accurate shooting in such crowded darkness would not be easy.

Whitey stopped, satisfied he'd found the proper graves. Again he offered his obscene prayers as he waved his hands over the victims. The other men unstrapped the young man as he struggled. I clutched the handle of my cart. The girl screamed through the tape covering her mouth. The men lifted the young man from the cart. He struggled as best he could, but the tape held him tight. Three men struggled to force him into the cramped grave carved from the side of the wall. They punched him until he lost his bearings. After that, they had no trouble easing him into his grave. Whitey said his prayers throughout in a language I didn't recognize.

I realized that in the chaos of getting the young man ready for sacrifice, there were no eyes on me at the moment. I put my hand on the girl's shoulder and gently squeezed. She craned her neck to see that it was me, the one who had offered a friendly look earlier. I winked, perhaps going overboard to let her know I was on her side. I carefully released the ratchet securing the strap, and it went loose. She didn't react to it, so I knew she played it cool.

They had the boy in the grave. The men chanted. Their noise obscured the sound of me using my keys to slice her taped bonds. She slid off the cart and stepped behind me. It was going to happen any second, whatever it was. I had to act. I lunged forward and quick-as-you-please took the gun from a man's belt. I stepped back into position before he realized what I'd done.

Now running on pure instinct, I fired twice. The shots were bright and booming, ringing my ears and blinding me and the others for a second. When my vision cleared, two men were on the ground, one writhing in pain, the other still.

Whitey, Mr. Philip and the others glared at me in shock and fury.

"What are you doing?" Mr. Philip asked.

"You cannot escape, you fool!" Whitey said.

"Get him out of there," I said, referring to the young man.

Whitey looked into the grave. His lips spread into a satanic grin as he looked back to me.

"It's too late for him, boy."

I glanced into the grave. A thick root had already burst from the dirt ceiling above him and pierced his chest. The root pulsated as it sucked away his blood. He shriveled, turned white, and died in seconds. The girl screamed and shook her head. I worried my limbs would go limp. A cramp seized my stomach. I assumed it was revulsion at the murder I had just witnessed. With dread I realized where the tree's fruit got its dark, red juice.

The men came forward. I shot another one. That was three rounds from the revolver. Only three shots left and still six opponents stalking us.

"You can't kill all of us," Whitey said.

Two of them drew their own pistols.

"You don't have enough ammunition," he said.

"True," I said. "So which three of you will it be?"

Whitey laughed, as did the others. "My boy, we have sworn our very lives to Almighty Gamorra. Death is but a door to us. A door to a place of eternal reward."

I fired again, this time hitting Whitey in the chest. He dropped with a gasp. The others froze.

"Go!" I hissed.

She grabbed a fallen torch and ran.

I picked up the cart and jammed its top and bottom against the walls, horizontally. I fired one more shot, heard a scream, and ran. Shots flashed from their guns and pings off the earthen walls of the tunnel as I fled. The earth rumbled and shook. I worried the walls would cave in. My heart leapt at the sound of a low growl like that of an angry old hag. Another stomach cramp doubled me over, but I recovered and quickly caught up to the girl.

"I don't know which way to go!" she said.

"There's only one way out," I said. "Just keep moving forward!"

Flickering ambient light from our pursuers' torches followed us. Roots abruptly darted out from the walls, trying to impale us. Four men remained to chase us, if my math was correct. I had one round left. The driver waited with the truck. Maybe luck was on our side.

The tunnel exit came into view just as our hunters rounded the last corner behind us. I looked back to see Mr. Philip raise a pistol at me with an unrecognizable look on his face. Four roots tore out of the walls and impaled his body. He convulsed and shriveled to a dead man almost immediately. Mother Gamorra was mad at everyone.

We broke out of the tunnel as it collapsed into the remaining men and ran into the fresh air and moonlight. The driver stood by the truck, puzzled by the earthquake. He slowly glanced at us. By the time he realized something had gone wrong and had stiffened up to resist, I had put my last bullet through his head.

I climbed behind the wheel as the girl got into the other side. No keys in the ignition. Of course. I dove out and searched the driver's pockets and found them. My stomach flared up again, this time so bad I worried I would pass out. It subsided just enough so I could move, but the pain remained. I returned to the truck to start it. We pulled away just as the cliff wall came down. The ancient manual transmission was a struggle, but I quickly adjusted.

By moonlight I found the road going up to the tree. I dreaded passing the evil giant, but I knew no other way out. The steep incline of the hill road was almost our undoing, as my driving skill with the old truck was barely adequate. We crested the hill though, and the young lady screamed when she saw the tree.

It was tall before, but now, the branches unfurled and reached a full twenty stories into the air. The branches waved and slammed at the ground as I did my best to avoid the lethal blows. The moan I'd heard earlier was now an ear-splitting shriek of cosmic rage. Roots tore thorough the ground, upending gravestones. Some of the roots had skeletons and bodies still skewered upon them. My companion prayed silently to herself. I hoped she prayed to the God more powerful than Gamorra.

I swerved, sped up, slowed down, and did all I could to get out of that field. The pain in my stomach was steady and unrelenting. Sweat poured down my face and soaked my clothes as I tried to ignore it for the benefit of our escape.

We entered the forest road. Only then did we dare to look back. Our timing was perfect. The entire field undulated and rippled as countless roots blasted out of the ground. The tree branches flailed and raged at the stars. Then the ground began to collapse into the thousands of graves below it. The cratering earth drew closer to us, and my companion urged me to drive faster.

It was our good fortune that the truck was well-maintained. There was no reason to look back again. The crumbling ground would catch up to us and swallow us, or we would escape.

Stopping at my uncle's house was out of the question. I had little doubt it wouldn't exist by morning. We sped through Main Street as the townspeople—fully morphed into vampiric creatures enraged with our sacrilege—attacked the truck. Even as monsters they were no match for a diesel truck. We escaped and drove straight out onto the county road. Only then did we look back once more to see the buildings and houses of Gamorra Fields sink into the earth with her citizens under a terrifying cloud of dust and smoke.

The road went flat and straight. We caught our breath. She ceased her prayers and kissed the crucifix on her necklace. Her body relaxed. Mine could not. My stomach cramps did not relent. I tried to make sense of what it could be. The closest comparison was to hunger pangs. I reasoned the extreme stress and lack of eating in the past twenty-four hours had caught up to me. A roadside burger would put me right, I hoped.

"I'm Dale, by the way," I said.

"Cassie," she said.

We shook hands, laughing nervously at the strangeness of our introduction.

Only at sunrise did we feel secure enough to stop. I stopped at the same roadside diner/gas station I had visited on my way up. Again I met by the nice lady and the bag boy. She saw our distress and provided us some water and food.

The girl and I sat at an outside table. The villagers kidnapped her, she told me. She didn't know the young man. Not his name or where he was from. No way to track down his family to inform them, even anonymously. We talked about whether to inform the police. Considering the magnitude of the disaster that took Gamorra Fields, it seemed obvious there would be a massive law enforcement response. Considering the complicity of the local sheriff to the evil deeds, we decided to go our own ways and try to forget.

Throughout our conversation, my stomach pains worsened. I tried to hide it, but the girl quickly caught on to my sweating and grimacing and rocking back and forth. Her kindness after all she'd been through moved me. I realized that I desired her badly. Only not in any kind of sexual or romantic way. It was hard to quantify. She sensed it was time for us to part.

Luckily I had my wallet in my pocket. Anything I left in the house was gone. I withdrew enough cash to get us both bus tickets home. She told me she hadn't been gone long enough to arouse any suspicion from her loved ones. As far as she was concerned, once she boarded the bus, she would toss Gamorra Fields from her mind forever.

Her bus arrived first. We shared a tight hug. I held it longer than was comfortable for her. Again, I had desires for her. She was ready to get away from me. She thanked me again and hurried onto the bus.

I had some time to kill, so I walked the aisles of the grocery. My stomach cried out in flaring pain for relief. None of the aisles I passed had anything that looked promising. I came to the jelly section. Along with the usual big-name brands was Gamorra Apple Jam. The sight of the narrow jar and its bright red contents caught me short.

The jam had worldwide distribution, the recently deceased Mr. Philip had bragged to me. Whitey's sermon said the seeds had fallen from space centuries ago, and a bloodthirsty entity had established a ritual of devotion and sacrifice among the locals. Their unique fruit was fed with human blood. They processed the apples and sent the product out into the world to spread its unholy virus.

The crisp cool flavor of the hard apple cider came to mind. I shook my head at my stupidity. Not one but three bottles of cider did I pour down my throat, infecting myself with their ancestral curse. For how long? I shuddered to speculate.

I could eat food, of course, as they did. But I would always require something more if I wanted my stomach to find rest.

The kind lady and the bag boy were back to work, lost in their duties. I studied them both. Her, a middle-aged woman with a robust figure. He, a strapping lad with an athletic frame. Plenty of what I needed flowed through both. My bus would not arrive in time to save them. The boy first, I think, while I still have most of my adult strength.

I walked away from the shelves and toward them. I thought I was hungry, but I was wrong.

I was thirsty.

Your Father's a Monster

Dr. Colin Wood returned home from his office later than usual. He hung up his coat, set down his briefcase, and looked around for his family. The handsome old house looked empty. The dining room was clear. A ripple of guilt tugged at his chest. He'd missed dinner, and he hadn't called. It was inconsiderate not to let loved ones know of your whereabouts at all times. Especially in the dark atmosphere that had overtaken the world. It wasn't impossible to stay safe, but one had to be crafty and smart. Dr. Wood was both.

The house wasn't silent. Classical music filled each room through a speaker system he had wired himself. They used to enjoy the silence, but there was too much outside noise anymore—loud vehicles, fights, gunshots, screams—and roars. For sanity's sake there was constant sound of some kind in their house and most others.

There was a plate filled with helpings from that evening's meal in the refrigerator, which made him feel worse. He microwaved the plate. Stella shuffled in, wearing cotton pajamas.

"Sorry I'm late, Dear," he said, giving her a kiss on the cheek, which she received with a smile.

"You didn't call, Mister," she said. "I've been worried."

"Again, sorry. Lots of emergencies today. Had to reschedule some appointments," he said. "So by the way, I'll be late tomorrow."

"So it goes. How was the ride home?"

He shrugged. "No different from usual."

"How many of them threw things at the car?"

"Four. A slow night."

"It's too late to open up a new discussion about moving—"

"And also too late to offer a rebuttal about how there's nowhere to run . . ."

"So I won't. You know how I feel about this. Just wanted to drop it into your mind to sleep on."

"So noted. Where's Mary?"

"Not home yet."

"Has she called?"

"Not yet. Not that you're in any position to get indignant."

"It's different."

"Why? Because she's a woman and you're a man?"

"Because I'm twice her age and twice her size."

"She's a smart girl," Stella said. "And we're not ready to spend all our time behind locked doors. Not yet. Besides, she's with a group of friends in the safe zone, and it's not all that late. You worry wart."

"She took her pistol?"

"Of course."

"And the proper bullets?"

"Do we store any other kind?"

"Good," he said. "I'll feel better when I'm fed."

"Want to watch some TV while you eat?"

They settled onto the couch. Dr. Wood ate his meal while Stella sat with him. They chatted as the television droned. The sounds of chaos from unstable parts of the city still reached the relative gated safety of the Woods' neighborhood. In was on evenings like this that Colin congratulated himself on his decision to become a doctor.

The show and the doctor's meal were half-over when the doorbell rang. Stella rose to answer it.

"Remember not to open the door until you know who it is," he said. "Use the monitor."

"So glad you're here to tell me these things," she said on the way out.

He scooped up the last of his dinner and wiped his mouth. Stella returned.

"It's a young man," she said. "Says he's hurt and needs help."

"Do we know him?"

"No."

"Is he one of them?"

"Hard to tell."

"Does he look like he's really hurt?"

"You're the doctor," she said. "Maybe you could make the long journey to the front door?"

He rolled his eyes and went to the front door. The monitor screen by the door showed a young man of about twenty. Sweat covered his face. A thick beard covered his mouth and jaw. He slumped against the porch wall.

"Yeah, he looks hurt," Colin said.

He pressed the intercom button. "What's wrong, son?"

The young man flinched at the doctor's voice.

"I need help, sir!" the youngster said. "I've been shot!"

"Oh my," Stella said. "Should I call an ambulance?"

On the monitor, Colin watched the young man collapse to the ground.

"At the way things are going now? Might take them an hour to show up."

Colin opened the door. "I'll stabilize him if I can and drive him to the hospital."

The young man groaned and writhed on the pavement as he held his abdomen. Colin knelt at his side.

"Who shot you?" Colin asked.

"Didn't see 'em. God, it hurts!"

"Shot just the one time?"

The young man nodded. Colin turned to his wife.

"Stella, set a tablecloth across the dining room table. Hurry!"

She ran to follow his instructions. Colin looked around to make sure he wasn't being snared in some kind of trap. The darkness surrounding his house and neighborhood hid no threats as far as he could tell. He helped the young man to his feet and guided him inside, shutting and locking the door behind them.

Stella had the dining room table ready. She helped get him onto the table. Colin tore the injured youngster's shirt away. The Woods saw the mass of hair covering the young man's body, then looked at each other. They stepped away from the table and out of earshot.

"He's one of them," she said.

"Most everybody has the genetic marker."

"But is he fighting it or letting it take him over?"

"I don't know, but he's here and hurt and I'm a doctor. Get me a mixing spoon, please."

When she came back with a wooden mixing spoon, Colin placed it across the young man's mouth. Stella also brought a handful of zip ties.

"Not a bad idea," Colin said.

They had the young man's hands tied to dining room chairs before he realized it.

"Bite on the spoon," Colin said to him. "This is going to hurt."

The young man grimaced, but he did as ordered. He bared his teeth and chomped on the spoon as Colin dug into the wound to check the damage. His eye teeth were twice as long as they should have been, but neither made a comment.

"Your bag," Stella said as she put his medical kit on the table.

"Looks like it went through clean," Colin said. "Good thing you have love handles, son."

Colin pointed at the network of black spider-like lines sprouting away from the bullet hole. Stella saw them and frowned at Colin, not understanding. He mouthed the word *silver*. Stella understood.

Colin took gauze padding from his kit. He pressed the padding into the wound.

"Press down on this," he said to Stella, who rushed over to apply pressure on the wound.

Colin monitored the bleeding for a few minutes.

"Looks like the bleeding is slowing down," Colin said.

He gave the young man a shot of morphine.

"Taking him to the hospital?" she asked.

"Just let me wash my hands."

"What about the police?"

"Are you kidding? They allow this anarchy to fester," Colin said. "I'll get him to the hospital, then I'll call and our job is done. The police take their time. So will we."

"They won't accept him at a safe zone hospital," Stella said. "And you cannot leave the safe zone."

Colin thought about that and nodded. "I'll get him as far as the zone border and summon an ambulance from there. Not very doctorly of me, but—"

"You've already done more than what's expected."

Colin left the room to wash up. Stella looked down at the young man. His eyes fluttered open, looking coherent as the morphine dulled his pain. His face relaxed. His head rolled toward her and their eyes met. She smiled. His eyes dropped down her her chest. She wore no bra under her thin cotton top. His smile was unsettling. Stella was uncomfortable. Colin returned, drying his hands.

"Let's see the wound," he said.

Stella lifted her hands from the young man's body and crossed her arms over her chest.

"The bleeding has slowed," Colin said. "I think you'll make it, son, but we'd better get you to the hospital and get you patched up. Can you sit up?"

The young man shook his head. Stella exhaled. She wasn't eager to unfasten his hands just yet.

"You need some more rest," the doctor said.

The young man returned to sleep. Colin turned to Stella. "I might call an ambulance after all. By the time he's ready to move, it might actually be here."

Colin ran to the front door to get his jacket from the coat tree. As he dug through the pockets for his phone, he heard a commotion from just outside. He checked the monitor.

A car had parked in his driveway. A man and woman pulled an unconscious young girl from their car. She was young. Her dress was ripped to pieces. It looked like—

"Mary!" Colin yelled as he opened the door and ran outside.

"Colin!" shouted the man.

It was John and Olivia, neighbors from down the street. "What happened?"

Colin gathered his daughter in his arms and carried her to the house. Stella appeared at the front door. Her mouth dropped open in shock at the sight of her daughter. Mary's eyes were swollen shut. Blood trickled from her nose and mouth. Spots of blood marked her arms and legs and bare feet. A row of deep gashes lined her chest.

"Olivia and I found her lying on the sidewalk, just blocks away," John said. "She's breathing."

"What happened?" Stella asked as they brought her in.

"Mary's been hurt," Colin said. "Looks like it was one of them."

He rushed up the stairs, taking Mary to her room. Stella watched him go up the stairs in disbelief. Then she snapped to, grabbed Colin's medical bag and followed him.

She looked into Mary's room as Colin checked her wounds. Colin reached for the bag. Knowing better than to get in Colin's way or get him agitated, she watched from the doorway. John and Olivia appeared behind her.

"What happened to her?" she asked them quietly. "Was she awake when you found her?"

"Barely," John said.

"We were on our way home," Olivia said. "We saw some sort of fight."

"We almost turned around to avoid it," John said.

"But at the last minute we saw it was a girl being attacked," Olivia said. "We couldn't turn away."

"Was them? Those things?" Colin asked.

John looked at the girl's wounds. "Had to have been."

"Then they're in the safe zone," Stella said. "God help us."

"The world's gone crazy," Olivia said.

"Colin? Will she be okay?" Stella asked.

"Substantial bleeding," Colin said, struggling to keep his voice calm. "Clawed and beaten. Maybe worse, I don't know yet. Pulse is steady. She'll live. Will she be okay? We'll have to see."

"Did they . . . did they . . ."

"I said I don't *know*, Stella," Colin said. "That kind of examination will have to take place at the hospital."

John and Olivia slipped away to give them privacy.

"So much for a safe zone," Stella said. "Now we'll be prisoners in our home."

"At least we'll be safe," Colin said.

"Our daughter's blood has been spilled in our home," she said. "It's worse than a prison."

Colin grunted in anger. It was an odd sound. Stella frowned and studied him. He rubbed his forehead. She softened her tone.

"How long 'til she wakes up?" Stella asked.

"She has a concussion. Let's get her to the hospital."

"Wait," Stella said, causing Colin to freeze. "What about her gun? Why didn't she use it?"

"Those things attack fast from out of the dark. Maybe they jumped her so fast she couldn't get it out of her purse."

They watched each other for a few seconds, then turned to look at Mary. Her purse was still slung around her shoulder. Colin cut the purse strap and dug through it.

"No gun," he said. "You're sure she took it?"

"I always insist."

Stella sat by Mary as Colin went downstairs.

"John," Colin said as he came down. "This might sound odd, but did you find a gun near Mary?"

John and Olivia exchanged a glance. "Didn't think to search for one."

"I know it might not be safe out right now, but could you go back and make a quick check?"

"Sure. We'll be right back."

They left. Colin sighed at the awful turn the night had taken. He returned to the dining room where the young man slept on the table.

Colin checked his pulse, then his breathing. His beard looked smaller than before. Or maybe Colin's memory was faulty. Who memorizes the thickness of a man's beard? He shook it off. Satisfied his patient was stable, he returned to Mary's room.

Stella kept watch. Her body relaxed and the shakes went away. Tears silently rolled down her cheeks.

"How could this happen?" she asked.

"The madness is closing in," Colin said. "Odds are this was going to happen to one of us."

"Why not me, then?" Stella asked.

"Or me."

"You remember the suppression protocols?" Stella asked.

Colin grinned in spite of his anguish. "It's not like you to use such clinical terms."

"Too much time spent with medical professionals, I suppose," she said. "Let's get old-fashioned like our grandparents and call them the Given Laws."

"They worked for a while, more or less."

"Now they're out of favor."

"And look at the results."

Stella stared at Mary's swollen face in a daze. "We've tried to deny the good it did us. Generations have tried to deny it. Those who came before had the luxury of denying it. Life was good and bountiful. We let ourselves believe the Laws had nothing to do with it. Well, it's not so good anymore. We've lost our capacity to care for each other. We hate so easily. The monsters are unchained now. It's always been free to manifest, of course, but now it's out for real in a way it hasn't before."

"Are you asking me if it's time to bend the Laws?" Colin asked.

"Would it be bending the Law if you're defending what it stands for? What options are left?"

"I'm not sure I'd know how to do what you're suggesting."

"Neither do I."

"Mary needs to go to the hospital," Colin said. "So does our guest. Hell with it. I'll drive them. I don't even trust the ambulance, and all the good cops have quit."

The doorbell chimed. Colin left the room before Stella could say any-more. He opened the front door to let in John and Olivia.

"I'll be damned, Colin," John said as he held out a silver revolver. "Here it is! Not three feet from where we found her."

Colin took the weapon and turned it over in his hands. He released the barrel and checked the cartridges. A single round had a depression from the firing pin. He took out the casing—the bullet was gone.

"She got off one shot," he said.

"Did she shoot the mugger?" Olivia asked.

Colin stared at the empty casing, then slowly turned to the direction of the dining room. John and Olivia followed him as he marched to the dining table to look at the young man. He still slept.

"Who's this?" Olivia asked.

Colin caught them up on what had happened before they arrived.

"Holy cow," John said.

"You think this is the one who attacked Mary?" Olivia said.

Colin stared at the sleeping young man. "I'm sure the police will . . ."

He looked at John and Olivia, sheepish. "Listen to me, talking stupid."

"We understand," Olivia said. "Who knows what to do anymore?"

The doorbell chimed. Colin stood up straight, tension in his face. "Now what?"

The couple followed Colin as he checked the monitor. There were three people, two men and a woman, all about the same mid-twenties age as the young man.

"How do they look?" John asked.

"Normal enough," Colin said. "If we can agree on what normal means."

"They sure seem scared," Olivia said. "I wonder if they saw the thing that attacked Mary."

Colin stared at the monitor in silence. The doorbell chimed again. The group looked terrified. Stella came down the stairs.

"Colin?"

Colin pressed the intercom button. "What is it?"

The others winced at the gruffness in Colin's voice.

The tallest of the two men leaned toward the intercom.

"Please, mister! Please let us in. They're coming over the security fence!"

"Who are you?"

"I'm Craig. This is Kadie and Jerry! Please! It's not safe!"

"Are you from the zone?" Colin asked.

"Does that really matter?" John asked. "They need shelter."

Colin glared him into silence.

"Yes! Our last name is Trillo! We're from the southwest sector of the zone."

Colin turned to the others. "I've never heard of any family in the zone named Trillo. You?"

Nobody had.

"We have a moral responsibility here, Colin," John said.

"Then take them into your home," Colin said, exploding. "My daughter's upstairs, savaged! And chances are good I saved the life of her attacker!"

John and Olivia stepped back.

"Take it easy," John said.

"No lectures on moral responsibilities," Colin said.

"All right."

Colin placed his hand on the doorknob, his other on the deadbolt switch.

"Everyone that comes into this house is on a tight leash," he said.

He pulled the door open. The trio outside rushed in, gushing their thanks, although mildly taken aback at Colin's icy demeanor.

"You said you were attacked?" Colin asked.

"By those things," Craig said.

"Good thing we can run fast," Kadie said.

Jerry started to speak, but Craig cut him off. "You're real kind folks."

"Trillo, right?" Colin asked. "Never heard that name. From the zone you said?"

Something dark flashed across Craig's eyes. Only Colin saw it. Craig kept his grateful disposition, though.

"Yeah, Trillo," Craig said. "We've lived in the zone since I was a kid."

"In that case, I'm glad you made it here," Colin said.

Their relief seemed deeper than that of people seeking shelter, but again, only Colin noticed it.

"Do you have family at home?" Colin asked. "I'll call them. We might even be able to get you safe passage there. We have emergency streets for this sort of situation, you know."

Craig couldn't keep the worry out of his face this time. Everyone saw it.

"No one's home," he said, a little too quickly. "Really, if we could just wait this out here, that would help. I'm sure this will all blow over. The police squads should be storming through here any second."

"Yes, I'm sure we'll be overwhelmed soon," Colin said.

Craig nodded, smiling. His eyes didn't smile.

"Let's go into the TV room," Stella said. "Colin will show you the way. I'm going to go check—"

A look from Colin.

"—on the security cameras. You all go in. I think there's a ball game on."

Everyone filed into the TV room.

"Sit where you like," Colin said as everyone took a seat.

He turned on the TV. A football game no one cared about flickered to life. John and Olivia sat in chairs along the perimeter of the room, looking unsure if they should stay or go.

"Is anyone hungry?" Colin asked.

Jerry and Kadie declined.

"Yeah, we should eat," Craig said. "It's been a while and we should get something in our bellies."

"Be right back," Colin said as he left the room.

Craig looked at John and Olivia and smiled. "You folks live here, too?"

"No," John said. "We live . . . a couple of streets over."

"Cool."

John nervously looked away. Craig kept Olivia in his sights until Colin returned with meat and crackers.

"Nothing fancy," he said. "But it'll stop the rumbling."

Once everyone had started on the food, Colin left and returned with sodas. With food and television, everyone had plenty of distraction to avoid each other.

"Do you three go to a Temple of the Law?" Colin asked the visitors.

They froze. They fidgeted. Jerry was about to answer. Craig cut him off again.

"Yeah. Yeah, sure. All people of sophistication do."

"People of sophistication?" Colin said, laughing. "I like that."

Craig's eyes went dark, but he showed his best good-natured smile. John and Olivia exchanged an uncomfortable look.

"Which temple do you prefer?" Colin asked.

Craig shrugged. "We're between temples at the moment."

"It happens," Colin said. "Don't mean to pry. I just recently had conversation about the Given Laws. You know of those, of course."

"Of course," Craig said. "The pillars of civilization."

"The same," Colin said. "Anyway, the conversation was about whether the laws were obsolete, or more needed than ever."

Silence.

"What do you all think?"

John cleared his throat. "I think the laws are useful, but they need balance against expanding knowledge as we go forward."

"They're fluid, then?" Colin asked.

"I suppose so," John said.

Craig shook a finger at John. "Fluid. I like that. Sure, that's how I see it."

"You'd argue against a strict interpretation of the laws."

"Sure. I don't like strictness."

"You prefer the lack of strictness swirling around us?" Colin asked.

"Colin—" Olivia started.

"Hey, man, I don't want to argue," Craig said. "But just so I'm clear, you a strict one?"

Colin shrugged. "Just been giving it some thought lately."

"I think when you make people choose between two extremes, they end up choosing an extreme," Craig said.

"Profound," Colin said. "Let me show you something."

Colin rose and led the group into the dining room. He entered quickly so he could see the trio's expression when they saw the young man tied to the table. The surprise was too great for them to hide.

"You know him," Colin said.

Jerry and Kadie looked to Craig, who sneered at Colin.

"We saw them bring the girl back here. Where is she?" Craig asked. "I wasn't done with her."

Olivia gasped and ran for the front door. Craig and the others underwent an instantaneous transformation. Hair, drooping ears, fangs, and hair covering their bodies. In a fingersnap, they became three werewolves. Kadie growled and rushed at Olivia, grabbing her with long talons and bringing her back to the dining room.

John and Olivia cowered in the corner near Colin, who stared at the trio with contempt.

Craig's canine mouth spread in an awful, mocking grin. His voice lowered to a sinister, sonorous tone. "Now answer me. Did the girl make it back? Tell me and I'll leave her just this side of survival. Don't make me have to search."

Colin, stone-faced, stepped out of the dining room and into the front hallway, still in view of the dining room.

"Stella!" he called up.

She appeared at the top of the stairs, smiling.

"She's awake! Sitting up!"

Her smile faded at Colin's grim face.

"What's wrong?"

"Come down. Bring Mary."

"Colin?"

"Do it!"

An agonizing thirty seconds later, Stella reappeared with Mary. She looked weak, but stronger than Colin had expected.

"Daddy?"

"Hi, Sweetie."

"What's going on?" Stella asked.

"It'll be okay," Colin said. "We're about to settle a debate."

Craig stepped into the hallway. Stella and Mary screamed.

"Come down and join us," Craig said, his voice low and guttural.

Everyone returned to the crowded dining room. Colin stood in front of his family.

"Lots of blood in this room," Craig said to his panting companions. "Let's make sure we share. Jerry!"

Jerry looked at him through dumb-dog eyes.

"Make sure Kadie gets some."

Jerry nodded.

"I want that woman," Kadie said, pointing at Olivia, who gasped.

"Can I ask a question first?" Colin asked.

Craig waited. Colin pointed to the young man on the table, whose canine features had manifested again, probably due to the others.

"Mary, is this the one who attacked you?"

Mary nodded, surprised and afraid. Craig chuckled.

"We let him have a go at her first," Craig said. "But he is young and stupid."

"Caught off guard, you mean," Colin said as he pulled the pistol from his back pocket and quickly pumped three bullets into the young man, killing him.

Everyone jumped and shouted in surprise. The werewolves readied to spring, but stopped short when Colin leveled Mary's pistol at them.

"Silver bullets," Colin said.

"Not enough rounds to stop us all," Craig said.

"I'm afraid you're correct," Colin said.

Colin's eyes turned blood red and his body shook.

"Daddy?" Mary asked, alarmed.

"Colin! No!" John screamed. "Don't lower yourself to this!"

Craig and the others saw what was happening, but their fear of the gun held them back.

"Do it," Colin said to John. "Or watch her die."

"I will not sink to their level!" John said. "That's not who I am!"

Colin exploded into full werewolf manifestation as quickly as the others had. He was taller and even more terrifying than any of the three. Jerry tried to run. Colin put the final two bullets into him and he fell to the floor to die.

Colin shielded his family as he and Craig growled at each other like rival junkyard dogs. Kadie rushed at John and Olivia. John, refusing to transform, fell away under a flurry of dagger-like claws. He hit the wall hard and bounced to the carpet. He made feeble attempts to save Olivia, but Kadie beat him dizzy until he could only watch Olivia die.

Colin and Craig clashed over the dining table. The two monsters brawled like two grizzly bears. Kadie rose from Olivia's body, blood dripping from her maw as she sized up Mary and Stella.

Colin, seeing that, held off Craig with one beefy arm as he took Kadie by the throat. Mary and Stella watched, wondering how it would turn out. Stella turned to Mary.

"Remember that we have always loved you more than life," she said.

"What? Mom?"

Stella became a werewolf in an eyeblink, her fur silver and dark gray. Kadie was too surprised to react before Stella tore her head off. Craig, knowing they outnumbered him, backed away from the fight, stepping over John, who cradled his wife's body.

"So much for the Given Laws," Craig said.

Colin and Stella closed in.

"The laws were not meant to protect you, filth," Colin said.

They rushed at Craig as he lunged for the front door. Each one seized an arm. Craig was no match for the double attack. The couple stabbed and slashed with their talon claws, taking little damage in return. Colin tore his opponent's arm free. Craig roared. The fight went out of him. He staggered back as Colin and Stella stalked him, deciding on how to finish him. He bumped against a wall and slid down, returning to human form by the time his butt hit the floor.

Mary, hearing the end of the battle, stepped into the hall to see the beaten Craig with her werewolf parents standing over him. Craig started at the bleeding stump where his arm had been. He was savaged, defeated. He rolled his gaze toward Mary.

"Your father's a monster," Craig said. "And your mother. Like me. Look at them."

"This is how you beg for mercy?" Mary said. "They had it forced out of them. You chose it. You waste blood. My father preserves it."

"Typical blinkered idiot arguing from nihilism," Colin said.

Colin stood over his vanquished enemy, his mighty chest heaving as he caught his breath. With unwavering yellow eyes he watched the pathetic, mortally wounded Craig.

"What do you think I should do now, Mary?" Colin asked.

"Make the world a better place, daddy."

Craig screamed, his terror escaping in his final moments as Colin darted at him with the speed of a snake. Craig's eyes widened as Colin's jaw clamped hard on his throat, shaking him side-to-side like a dog with a rat. Only when Craig's head was free of his body did Colin still the attack.

They stared at Craig's dismembered body. A rustling sounded behind them. It was John, unsteady on his feet, the remains of Olivia in his arms.

"I want to take my wife home," John said.

"I see the contempt in your eyes, John," Colin growled. "Save it for the man in the mirror. You had a choice. You chose to bury your wife."

John looked down. Colin opened the front door. John froze.

Colin stepped out onto his front porch to see a gathering of were-wolves on his lawn. Their shock surpassed his own. They stepped back when they saw him. He marched fearlessly onto the grass and released an ear-splitting howl as he raised his massive, hairy arms to the moon. Then he waited, daring any of them to challenge him.

The other werewolves looked to each other, and slowly they mean-dered away, returning to human form. Colin nodded at John, who was now free to return home unmolested.

When Colin returned to his home and shut the door, he was in human form again, as was Stella. He gathered his family in his arms, and they wept with relief and joy. The first rays of the morning sun let up the ugly aftermath of their battle.

"Now what, Daddy?" Mary asked.

"Yes, what do we do with them?" Stella asked. "Should we call the police?"

They laughed.

"I'll build a fire in the back," Colin said.

When the fire raged, they tossed the bodies of the four intruders upon it and watched until they were ashes. They spent the day cleaning the mess from their walls and carpets. That evening, Colin and his family sat down together to a wonderful meal, served in fine china, with their best silver, wearing their Sunday best. By the next sunset, there was no sign that any of it had happened, other than the ash pile in their backyard.

Elijah's Ride

Elijah and Faith waited on a plush sofa in Dr. Misik's consulting room on Lennox Orbital Colony IV. His office faced Earth. The couple sat in silence, watching the oceans and continents pass by beneath wisping clouds below. Their fingers entwined just so as they held hands. He enjoyed the warmth of her hip as it touched his. Again, just so. After ten years of marriage, they knew the mutual comfort zone of every touch, every position.

Elijah took a deep breath, then wiped beads of sweat from his forehead. Faith lightly squeezed his hand in support.

"How long since the last one?" she asked.

"I don't remember exactly," he said. "But sooner than usual."

She didn't reply. The door whisked open with a hiss. Dr. Misik entered, carrying an electronic pad. The couple straightened up. They weren't nervous. They had most of the answers they sought already. This was a confirmation appointment. Part of the process. One of the last parts.

"Thank you for waiting, folks," Dr. Misik said. "How are you feeling now, Elijah?"

"Just a spell," Elijah said.

"More frequently than before, I'm guessing?"

"Yes."

Dr. Misik nodded. "Well, as you expected, the bio-scan results came back the same. That makes three consecutive bio-scans in agreement. According to the law, we can state with certainty your outcome."

"I'm going to die," Elijah said.

"That is the end game for those of us who refuse the enhancement," Dr. Misik said. "It is they who offer eternal life. Here, we do things the old-fashioned way, more or less. Technology is advanced enough to pinpoint your natural death date just as we can pinpoint your natural birth date."

"How long?" Faith asked.

"His heart will stop in approximately twenty-three hours."

They clutched each other's hand. There was no getting used to such news.

"And there's no available treatment?" Faith asked.

"Only the enhancement," Dr. Misik said. "And they will travel here if you decide to do it."

Faith looked at Elijah. He shook his head. She smiled, expecting that reaction.

"Elijah, as a certified medical doctor, I judge you to be of sound mind," he said. "I'm asking your wife, Faith, if she concurs. Do you?"

"He is of sound mind," Faith said.

"I've completed all the required scans," Dr. Misik said. "All possible treatments considered and ruled out. I hate to sound gloomy or insensitive, but I'm legally obligated to tell you this in the presence of your next-of-kin: You are going to die in twenty-three hours. Do you understand?"

"I understand," Elijah said.

"Is it your intention to refuse the enhancement?"

"I refuse the enhancement."

"Have you completed pod travel training?"

"I am so trained."

Dr. Misik entered Elijah's responses into a program on his pad. Elijah and Faith confirmed the information with a fingerprint scan.

"Very well. I have just transmitted pod authorization to the appropriate teams. They'll expect you at Dock 7A in twenty-two hours."

"Okay."

He handed Elijah a bottle of pills. "This should help with the spells for the rest of your time. Just a maintenance measure. They'll help keep your head about you until the end, but it won't stop what's to come."

Elijah took the bottle.

"Don't wait too long, if you want to take the pod journey," Dr. Misik said. "Otherwise, you'll risk dropping in a corridor or something. Sorry to be blunt, but I've seen it happen."

"I'll make sure he stays on schedule, Doctor," Faith said.

Dr. Misik stood and shook their hands. "An enhancement physician is on standby, should you have a last-minute change of heart. Otherwise, Godspeed on your way."

Faith had the farewell party ready to go. She wanted to leave the final consultation and go straight to Elijah's celebration of life. The orbital colony had staff available for just such a purpose. Once Elijah's scan indicated an imminent natural end of life, and that he had decided against the enhancement, they mobilized immediately.

"Let's get changed for your party while you're still up for it," she said.

They returned to their apartment. They undressed and selected nicer outfits for his farewell. As usual, Elijah was dressed and ready while Faith was still naked. She wore only her gold sandals as she stood before their closet. She turned to display two outfits.

"Which one?"

"I think you're good in what you're wearing," he said.

"That's for later. Come on. We're on the clock here."

"Okay, okay. The white one. You're already wearing the shoes for it."

She slipped into the snug gauzy, white jumpsuit and accented it with the gold jewelry he loved. Her hair cascaded down her bare shoulders. While she dressed, he dug into his own closet and brought out a dusty old wine bottle. He grinned.

"You've had that since we've been together," she said. "Whenever I asked what it was, you told me I had to wait until it's time."

"It's time," he said. "An ancestor purchased this in 1906. Back down on Earth."

"You don't say."

"They barely had cars then," he said. "Anyway, it became a tradition in our family that the firstborn of each generation would have a single toast from the bottle, cork it, then pass it on to the next generation."

She took the bottle and examined it. The bottle had an oval body and a long, fluted neck. The faded cream-colored label had almost peeled off. Ancient dust caked the grooves in the neck. She swirled it around, testing its fullness.

"Feels like it's almost empty," she said.

"This might be the last toast."

"Then what?"

"I don't know. The bottle becomes an heirloom, I guess. I hope."

"I'll keep it if your family doesn't want it."

He took the bottle and held it carefully. "The spirits in this bottle have washed down toasts and farewells and welcome-homes for over two hundred years. Seems appropriate I'll take the last toast."

"Since you'll be the last of your family to die, I suppose so."

They arrived to the banquet room to cheers and applause. Most of them were like Elijah and Faith, who refused the enhancement and were known as natural-agers. The variety of people present—young and old, dark hair and gray hair—was now an aberration in a populace made forever young by advanced technology. There were a few enhanced ones in Elijah's party, but most had declined the procedure.

Elijah smiled in approval at the feast Faith had arranged. All his favorite casseroles and desserts. Dr. Misik had told him it was fine to eat up before the pod journey, and Elijah did exactly that. He took his time to sample everything and ate until his stomach stretched his pants.

When the meal had died down, attendants came to clear away the remnants. After-dinner drinks were served. Elijah and Faith found themselves alone at the head table. He brought out the old wine bottle. He removed the cork and put the mouth of the bottle to his nose. The aroma of the red liquid was deep and full and still fresh.

"I can almost hear the laughter and tears," he said.

He poured wine into his glass. The bottle splashed empty with the glass half-full. He held the bottle upside-down until every last drop fell.

"I guess I'm the last one," he said.

"The end of an era," she said.

Elijah held the glass and took in the surroundings.

"My ancestral offering," he said. "Not sure of the best way to do it."

"You're overthinking it," she said. "Come on."

She led him to a magnificent floor-to-ceiling viewing window. It took up an entire wall. Planet Earth and the stars beyond provided a dazzling sight. Elijah's belly fluttered at the sight.

"Yes. This is the right place," he said, turning to her. "The right place and the right person."

Her smile was wide and beautiful. He wanted to tell her how her beauty was the only thing that could make him accept the enhancement. If she asked him to, it would be hard to say no. They had agreed early in their marriage to refuse enhancement, that they would take their love to the grave, like the great lovers of old. They had also agreed not to tempt each other away from that mutual decision.

"It never fails to take my breath away," he said.

"Earth? Or me?" she asked with a wink.

"Yes."

"It's only the beginning," she said. "There will be many beautiful things."

"I know. I wish we could see them together."

"I'll be along soon enough."

She watched him idly swirl the glass. "Are you ready?"

He pointed at Earth. "That's the Atlantic Ocean."

"I know."

"My ancestors made their living from it," he said. "They came from the northern lands. In ancient days, they were called 'men from the north.' Or 'Norsemen.' That's as far back as I was able to trace them."

He raised his glass. She likewise raised her glass of champagne.

"To the northern lands. To the ocean . . ."

Faith was as beautiful as he's ever seen her. It ached to look at her, but he did it anyway.

". . . to eternal love."

Alone together by the viewing window, witnessed only by Faith, Elijah drank the last of the ancestral wine. He held it in his mouth for a moment. He closed his eyes and swallowed.

"Well?" she asked.

"Wonderful," he said with a sigh.

"Don't be sad," she said.

"I feel many emotions at once. Nothing I anticipated about this day has borne out."

"That's because you're saying hello and goodbye at the same time."

He put his arm around her. They turned from the window and made their way into the heart of the party. Elijah loved to study the look and behavior of crowds. All were dressed as sexy and stylish as their bodies would allow, as if their bodies were canvas upon which to make art. The people were loud. There was much laughter and gaiety. People would smile and nod and wave at Elijah.

"I'm more excited than anxious," he said. "Is it wrong for me to be so eager for the end?"

"I would worry if you weren't."

"I just want to feel what's appropriate."

"Don't be self-conscious," she said. "Men of old have wondered for ages about where you're going. They eventually learned. As will you."

A girl of about nine or so and wearing a pretty dress crashed into Elijah, rocking him back a step.

"Daddy!" she said.

He chuckled, but before he could correct her, she held up an open book and pointed to the text.

"What's that word," the girl asked.

"I'm sorry, Sweetheart, but I'm not your—"

"Right here!" She was insistent. "What's that word?"

It was easier to play along than argue. Elijah squatted down next to her and looked at the book. "Uh, okay. Let's see here . . . um . . . the word is 'uppermost.'"

"Thanksbyeloveyou," she said as she snatched the book and ran into the crowd. She dove under a table and out. She darted around grown-up legs. Worried about her safety, he was about to scold her to slow down when he saw that none of the partygoers took notice of the young girl. He turned to Faith, who wore a knowing smile. He looked back and the girl had vanished.

"What was all of that? Who was she?"

"Remember what I told you? As you get closer, you will see things that others can't see. You'll see other futures. Other possibilities. Different realities will cross over with your own. Eventually, they'll all meet at your final destination."

"Was she really—"

"A part of you?" she asked.

"I meant a part of us."

"In another time, yes."

"That only makes things harder," he said.

She rubbed his back.

"Don't worry," she said. "There will be a coming together. You'll see her again. So will I."

Beads of sweat appeared on his forehead. He exhaled hard.

"Having a spell?" she asked.

"A little winded, but good. Just as Dr. Misik predicted."

"Do you need a pill?"

"One more ought to get me to the finish line," he said as he discreetly popped a little pill.

A young couple, Mark and Maryann, got up from their table to greet Elijah and Faith as they passed by.

"Hello, Elijah!" Maryann said. "We are so very happy for you!"

"Two of my oldest friends!" Elijah said. "I'm glad you came."

"We couldn't call ourselves lifelong friends if we missed this!" Mark said. "Faith, always a pleasure. You are beautiful."

The old friends laughed and reminisced as old friends so easily do. As the conversation wound down, Mark handed Elijah a book.

"That's for your journey," Mark said as Elijah examined it. "It's not exceptionally rare, of course—"

"But we know how much you like old things," Maryann said.

"It's not rare, but it's old!" Mark said.

"I'm an old soul, for sure," Elijah said.

"Well, we'll not keep you. Just wanted to say hello," Mark said.

"And to tell you we finally had our first bio-scans last week," Maryann said.

"And how did that turn out?" Elijah asked.

Their happy faces faded just a little.

"We got some news," Mark said. "Had some decisions to make."

"I bought a book for myself," Maryann said. "I won't be far behind you."

Elijah and Faith nodded as they knew what that meant.

"I see," Elijah said. "In that case, I wish you Godspeed on your journey, when it comes."

"And to you," she said.

Mark and Maryann said their goodbyes and moved on.

Faith noticed three newcomers enter the ballroom. They looked to be in their twenties. All of them wore clothing made from finely tailored, expensive fabric. Their skin was almost unnaturally clear. All had athletic builds.

"Your family is here," Faith said.

It was Joseph, Elijah's father, who came toward them with Jeanne, Elijah's sister and another man they didn't know.

"I have some people to talk to," Faith said. "I'll give you a minute."

She left him alone. Jeanne stopped and turned to speak to Joseph and the other man. Her body language suggested she wanted to speak to Elijah first. They stayed behind.

Elijah marveled at the sight of his older sister in her glittering silver dress. It was cut out from just under her breasts to below her navel. It was likewise open in the back. The dress hugged her figure close. Her enhanced, zero body fat muscular form was on display for all to notice. Notice they did. Not in judgment, but admiration. The enhanced were specimens to behold. She looked ten years younger than Elijah despite being five years older. The disapproval and unhappiness in her aquamarine eyes was evident. It pleased him to see her anyway.

"This is a wonderful surprise," he said.

"I had to see my baby brother."

"I had hoped to see you, too."

Jeanne looked around the gathering. "And these are your brothers and sisters in the faith?"

"You're just in time for the snake-handling," he said.

"I hope you're joking."

"We're not a religion, Jeanne. We're just like-minded people."

"Who refuse the enhancement?"

There was enormous pressure for everyone to accept the enhancement. Those who declined it were advised to prepare for these sorts of pressures from family and friends, so people like Elijah kept their patience and seldom got agitated.

"Yes, we have all refused and we show it," he said. "You, however, look wonderfully enhanced. My compliments."

"It's not just for vanity's sake," she said. "This may sound odd to you, but what Dad and I have done is the natural order of things."

Elijah frowned. "I thought I'd heard every possible pitch for the enhancement, but doing it to validate the natural order is a new one."

"Natural because it is the product of human minds," she said.

"Would you care for a list of unnatural things conceived of by the human mind?" he asked.

"Don't distract. I'm talking about the continuing experience of being human! Living. Being a family!"

"I cherish all those things," he said. "But it is only part of the cycle. A cycle which you deny. I can't."

"We're not helpless anymore," she said, urgency in her voice. "You can extend your cycle. You can have all the moments you want." She indicated Faith. "A lifetime of moments with her."

He looked at Faith, who stood out from the crowd as she spoke to other guests. Jeanne saw a hint of conflict in her brother.

"Don't go," she said. "Stay with us. Get her to stay."

"I didn't come to this decision lightly," he said. "I've studied more than you might know. Are you aware that there are no philosophical or religious traditions that call for what you've done?"

"Each new age brings with it new philosophies and perspectives," she said. "Do your ancient traditions call for bio-scans? Spaceships?"

Elijah shifted his stance and considered that. "I suppose not. But bio-scans and spaceships aren't people with souls. I don't claim to have all the answers. I draw the line where I feel I must."

"What if you're wrong?" she asked, winding down her appeal. "What if you wake up in a cold, black pit of nothing?"

"Then I won't worry, will I? But what about you? What if your actions will keep you forever from the numinous?" he said. "How much will you yield to technology to live forever?"

"I guess we've both thought about the unintended consequences," she said. "I just had to ask."

"I truly appreciate you asking me the question."

"And as usual, neither of us will bend," he said.

The laughed. Elijah removed a handkerchief and dabbed his moist forehead. Jeanne watched him take a deep breath and put her hand on his arm to steady him. He nodded his appreciation as the spell passed. He looked healthy again. She took his face in her hands. She smiled at him. He put his hands on her firm shoulders, knowing the effort it took for her to push down her sadness and reflect her love for him.

"I love you," she said. "No matter where you end up. You'll remember that?"

"I will. I love you, too. And think of me often. You'll have plenty of opportunities. It'll help."

Tears escaped her beautiful eyes as she turned away. Joseph and his companion saw her leave and took that as their cue to approach Elijah.

Jeanne composed herself as she went to the drink table. Faith found her, and they struggled through their usual awkward small talk. Heads turned at Jeanne's beauty. Only Faith was more beautiful. One man in particular studied Jeanne's appearance. He watched her rather obviously, not noticing how he himself stood out.

He looked close to fifty-years-old. His weathered face hid emotion. His hands were thick and large. He bore little resemblance to the fair men raised in space. Only those schooled in ancient history would recognize his dark blue pea jacket and seamen's cap. He looked lost, yet confident he was in the right place.

Faith noticed him and smiled. Jeanne frowned, unable to see the man in the pea jacket. Faith excused herself to talk to the man.

"Clarence?" she asked.

"Do I know you?" he asked. "I don't think I know you."

"I'm so glad you came!"

She kissed him on the lips. He chuckled at a kiss from a pretty lady.

"Are you the one who brought me here? I'm glad you did," he said. "This is amazing!"

She followed him to the large viewing window. He watched Earth floating beyond the glass. His face fell in awe.

"Look at that. By gum. My grandmother used to tell me stories of such possibilities. I guess she wasn't so crazy after all."

"She is a special soul, Clarence. A traveler. Like you."

"It's good to be with her again," he said. "Is the kid here?"

Faith motioned toward Elijah. Clarence saw him.

"Good lookin' kid. Comes from the McClain side. I can tell that right off. Should I talk to him?"

"Better to let him find you," she said. "Have some food. Make yourself at home."

Across the room, Elijah shook hands with his father. Joseph looked the same age as his daughter, Jeanne, due to both of them being enhanced in their early 20s. Joseph looked ten years younger than his son, Elijah. Such disparities made it difficult to tell the younger generations from the older.

"How are you, Dad?"

"Very well, thanks. I appreciate the invitation."

"I know you don't approve of my decision, so your coming here means a lot."

Joseph acknowledged that with a polite nod, then gestured to the man with them.

"Elijah, this is Dr. Portis."

Elijah shook hands with the doctor.

"I've asked him to join us because—"

"I know why he's here," Elijah said. "I'm not taking the enhancement."

"I respect that," Dr. Portis said. "Many people refuse at first."

"Then why are you here?"

"Dr. Misik is your physician, yes?"

"I saw him this morning," Elijah said. "Final scan. No change."

Joseph watched their conversation closely, particularly watching Elijah's reactions.

"Dr. Misik's reputation is beyond reproach, as is the accuracy of the genetic bio-scan. Have you considered an outside evaluation?"

"I'm not seeking a second opinion."

"It's an awfully big step, son."

"I have accepted my future, and I expect everyone else to accept it as well. The end date is conclusive. Twenty hours, give or take."

"But it doesn't have to be, as you well know," Dr. Portis said. He patted his briefcase. "The enhancement will prevent what is to come. It is permanent repair and maintenance. And I do mean permanent."

"Endless mornings," Elijah said in a sing-song voice. "Isn't that how the advertisements go?"

"Our motivation is the same as yours, Elijah," said the doctor. "To explore the unknown. To push back frontiers. One injection and every day from here on will be the first day of eternity."

Elijah considered that, wondering if those were words from an advertisement he had not yet seen.

"There are no 'days' in eternity," Elijah said. "Nor are there any doubts or questions."

"The certainty of another day versus the faith of what cannot be seen or heard?" Dr. Portis asked.

"Faith in the certainty of another day?" Elijah asked. He tutted and shook his head. "You act on your faith, Doctor. I'll act on mine."

The doctor had more to say, but Joseph motioned him to silence.

"Thank you, Doctor, but I think Elijah is firm in his commitment to his decision," Joseph said.

Thus dismissed, Dr. Portis nodded farewell to Elijah and joined Jeanne at the bar.

"I took the enhancement and stopped aging when I was a younger man than you," Joseph said.

"Obviously. By all rights you should be quite ugly by now."

"There are fringe benefits to the enhancement," he said with a wink and they laughed.

Joseph sighed, accepting that his son had chosen a different path. "Parting like this will give me many years to miss you. Just as I've had many years to miss your mother. She thought as you do," he said. "Part of your motivation, I suppose."

"Yes."

"I'll not forget either of you, even though it's hard for me to remember what years are."

"I would regret it if I set off without your blessing," Elijah said.

"Of course you have my blessing. A man's life is his own. I respect that."

"Thank you," Elijah said. "For all that I can remember, and all that I have forgotten."

"It was my duty," Joseph said. "My pleasure. My honor."

Joseph looked out the viewing wall. "I do envy you in a way. But the urge to see what comes next. It's too strong to resist."

"That's your right, Father," Elijah said. "I long to see what comes next, too."

"I suppose we each want that, in our own way," Joseph said. "You will say hello to your mother if you get the opportunity?"

"I hope it's the first thing I do."

"I believe I shall see her as well. I've read theories of the evolution we'll undergo. Stimulating stuff."

"Perhaps our paths will someday lead to the same destination," Elijah said.

"I hope so."

Elijah offered his hand. His father responded with a hug. Jeanne and

Dr. Portis saw this and returned to them.

"We'll be off then," Joseph said.

"Just a moment," Elijah said.

He jogged back to the table where he had dined and fetched the empty wine bottle. He returned to the group and gave it to Jeanne.

"It's empty," she said.

He grinned and shrugged.

"You might have a son or daughter someday," he said. "You might as well give them the bottle."

Jeanne hugged him tight. She was more at peace than before. With their goodbyes said, Joseph, Jeanne and Dr. Portis left the room. They would return to the hangar where they had docked, then board their shuttle for a return trip to Earth.

Faith saw them leave. When it looked as though Elijah had had adequate time with his thoughts, she called for the room's attention. Everyone quieted down and gathered around. Elijah joined them.

"Thank you for coming," she said. "We are here because we love Elijah. We love life. We honor the sacred cycle of birth, life, and death."

There were murmurs of agreement from the people. Clarence stood at the edge of the group and watched Elijah. He waited to see if Elijah would notice him. Elijah did catch a quick glimpse of Clarence, but he suddenly vanished from his sight, just like the little girl. Elijah wiped more sweat from his brow. Despite the medication, the symptoms grew worse. Time was short.

"Technology allows us to know the truth of our existence. Where we come from. How we end," Faith said.

Elijah felt winded again, but concealed it.

"Here we salute Elijah, who has chosen of his own free will to face eternity as did his forefathers—with courage and dignity."

Clarence appeared again with a glass of whiskey, nodding at those words.

"And now that sweet, sad hour is upon us. Elijah—"

Faith raised her glass. The others did likewise.

"When mist to rain and rain to sea. The circle that knoweth me. Mist to rain and rain to sea. The same is my wish for thee."

The gathered fell silent a moment to allow the words to settle in, then there were shouts of "hear! hear!" Someone applauded and everyone joined in. Faith went to Elijah. Another mild spell shook him. Her concern was quiet enough to avoid notice from anyone else. He smiled and nodded his assurance.

The crowd parted as they applauded. They formed a path to the exit. Elijah and Faith walked the path. Elijah shook hands with the men and received kisses from the ladies. At each person, he would pause for a second or two to discuss a moment from their relationship. He did this with every attendee until they were at the door. Then he turned and waved goodbye. The door whisked open, and they stepped through.

They stood in the quiet hallway.

"This silence brings it all into focus," he said.

He rubbed his forehead and exhaled. He leaned into her. She steadied him and then took his hand.

"Come on. One more thing before you go," she said.

They returned to their apartment. In the living room were seven women sitting in a circle. Barefoot and robed, they whispered to themselves. All communication and entertainment screens were dark, and the light in the room was low.

"They're praying for you," Faith said as she led him through the group and into the bedroom.

The only light came from small bundles of fiber-optic strands that hung from the ceiling. Faith guided him to the rustic antique bed. The wood frame was unshaped as if logs were hewn from a tree and immediately bolted together.

Faith sat him on the bed and undressed for him..

"My dizziness is gone," he said as he watched.

She laughed. "I'll try not to be offended."

"I'm feeling a better sensation."

"Good."

He undressed and she joined him on the bed. They kissed and touched.

"We could have an eternity of moments like this," he said.

"It will already be an eternity," she said.

"Leaving you will not be easy," Elijah said.

"We already live forever. In this moment," she said. "It's what the others don't understand."

"Let me remember," he said.

The next few hours were theirs.

Elijah later started awake in a mild panic, as if all that had happened were a dream. He heard the soft whispering of the praying women in the other room and knew that it was all still his reality. Faith slept peacefully beside him. The soft light on her skin gave her the golden glow of a goddess.

He rose from the bed and went into the bathroom for a shower. Faith's eyes fluttered open as he left the room.

Elijah stood in the shower and let the warm water run over his body. He watched the life-giving element run down his chest and arms and legs and swirl at his feet. He cupped water in his hands and poured it into his other hand. He knew space station water was imported from Earth. He enjoyed the caress of his home planet.

After his shower, he stepped in front of the full-length mirror, dripping wet. He flexed the muscles in his chest and arms, then his legs. He made fists with his hands, then stretched them open wide. He felt the texture of his skin. He ran his fingers through his hair. His tongue took inventory of his teeth. He sensed her presence at the door. She was there, wearing only a glowing sheen of sweat.

"It's perfect," he said. He flexed his arm and watched his bicep contract. "The body. The way it all works together. I never stopped to appreciate it before now."

He looked at his hands, feeling gratitude for how they had guided him through life.

"It's not a coincidence," she said. He frowned, not knowing what she meant. She went to him and stood next to him. Together they moved and flexed and took a new look at the function of their bodies. He continued his stretching as she ran her hands over his body.

"That all of this would come together to make you. That's what beauty is, you know."

He understood. For the first time in his life, Elijah felt beautiful.

She waited for him in the corridor. He emerged in a black tunic with a silver sash. Her expression puzzled him.

"I chose it yesterday," he said. "Didn't want to waste time deciding today."

"Are you sure you want to wear that?" she asked.

He looked panicked.

"It's a joke," she said. "Are you ready to go?"

He thought about that question and took a deep breath.

"Are you ready to go?" she asked again.

He nodded. "Yes. Let's go."

They walked hand in hand until they arrived at Docking Area 7a. They greeted a couple of well-wishers along the way. Near the dock entrance, they found Clarence by the door. They stopped in front of him. Faith watched Elijah, who felt a jolt of recognition.

"Do I know you, sir?" Elijah asked. "You look very familiar to me."

"We haven't actually met," Clarence said. "But we have, shall we say, common ancestors."

Elijah brightened.

"You know, it's funny. I watched us pass over the ocean a few minutes ago," Clarence said. "I lived my life there. Made my living from it. I had a large family. I often wondered how long it would continue, how far we would scatter."

Elijah understood. "I see. I wish you had shown up sooner. I have so much to ask you."

"Oh, don't worry. We'll do some catching up later. I have some people to introduce you to."

Elijah smiled at the man. "I guess the explorer spirit runs in our family."

Clarence cackled and gave Elijah a hearty swat on the shoulder.

"May the wind be at your back, my boy."

He tipped his hat to Faith and walked away, fading into the air before he reached the turn in the corridor. Faith nudged him along. They entered the dock.

It was one of the smaller docks. It was not like the large ones used for cargo ships and large passenger craft. This one was for small spacecraft like the round, one-person pod which sat in the center of the room. A dock attendant finished up a maintenance check of the tiny craft.

"I wish you could be with me," Elijah said.

"I'll be closer than you think," said Faith. "But you have to go the rest of the way alone."

"As do you," he said.

"I can do it if you can."

He held back his emotions. "Deal."

They kissed goodbye.

"Fare thee well," she said. "I love you."

"I love you, too."

She gave him a smile to remember her by, then turned and walked away. He watched her leave. She left the hangar, pausing at the door. She looked back. One more smile and wave, and she was gone.

He turned at the attendant's approach.

"Hello, Elijah," the attendant said. "My name is Paula. I'll be handling your launch."

"Nice to meet you."

"Do you remember your training?"

"I do."

"Any questions, then?"

"No, none that I can think of."

"There's a special room next to the control room if you need a minute."

"I'm ready to go now."

"Very good, sir. This way, please."

Paula led Elijah to the pod entrance, which stood open like a black metal jaw. He stepped up into the pod and took his seat. She leaned in and fastened his straps.

"Once the pod seals, the onboard computer will take over," Paula said. "There will be no more communication from our end. Unless, of course, you change your mind and choose to return. Is your decision final?"

"It is."

"Very well. Before I seal the pod, I must ask you this: Do you enter this pod of sound mind and of your own free will?"

"I do."

"Then I wish you Godspeed on your journey."

She ducked out of the pod and lowered the hatch. He heard a hiss and felt a slight popping in his ears as the craft pressurized. The control panels were designed for maximum ease of use. He had undergone training so he would be able to steer the craft should anything go wrong with the onboard computer. The controls flickered and beeped to life. The top, front quarter of the pod was structural glass, and through that he saw the docking doors pull apart to a blanket of stars. He sensed the docking area depressurize. A feminine voice came through the speakers.

"Are you comfortable, Elijah?"

It was clear and convincing enough to be a woman sitting next to him.

"I am, yes," he said. "To whom am I speaking?"

"I'm your onboard computer. You can call me Janet."

"Very well, Janet. I'm in your very capable . . . voice."

"Witty. The controls before you should look familiar. Do you remember your training?"

"Let's see . . . communications. Environment. Manual maneuvering. I think I can handle it if I need to."

"The manual controls are for emergencies only," Janet said. *"Otherwise, I will guide you. You may choose to turn around up to the very last second."*

"Understood."

He settled in and found the seat to be comfortable.

"You will now sense movement. Do not be alarmed."

The floor of the docking area moved forward. It extended out from the hangar doors like a tongue, protruding into space with the pod upon it. Elijah felt a tingling in his innards as he always did when entering space.

The struts holding the pod to the platform blew free. The platform rotated out from under the pod as it drifted free into space. One second later, the pod's modest thrusters fired. Elijah's ride had begun. He felt a slight push, then relaxed as the pod found its cruising speed.

Before him was the moon. Beyond that was the Sun, the neighboring planets, then eternity.

"I am coming home," he said.

As Elijah launched into space, Faith returned to their bedroom with a mix of peace and heaviness. The praying women kept up their vigil. She stood at the window. She caught sight of Elijah's pod, a black dot coasting against the glow of the moon.

The gravity engines gained speed quickly, soon manipulating space/time. The craft sped past the moon. Protective layers of glass saved him from the searing rays of the sun coming over the moon's edge. The pod rocketed into space faster and faster.

"There are plenty of entertainment choices for you," Janet said. *"Would you like to read, or perhaps hear a piece of music?"*

"I'm fine, Janet."

"Would you like to converse? I know many subjects."

"I'd like to be alone with my thoughts until the end. If you don't mind."

"Of course. I will remain silent."

The sensation came just as Dr. Misik had predicted. Elijah began to nod off. His dizziness returned, stronger than before. He had to take several deep breaths to catch up. He was only minutes away from destiny, if not seconds.

"No," he said to himself. "Not just yet."

He looked out at the stars. He knew the orbital colony—and Faith— was far behind him.

"Just a little longer," he said. "Just a little longer."

Faith lost sight of the pod.

"It's okay," she whispered.

Elijah stared wide-eyed as he entered a wonderland of the universe's grand show of magic. Before him was a vast canvas of planets and suns and nebulae. Waves and pools of colors and light. The universe had gathered her greatest beauty to welcome him here.

The pod started to bob as if he were on the sea. He tried to remember if Dr. Misik had predicted such a sensation. He couldn't remember.

His fatigue and dizziness and shortness of breath were gone. Forever. His skin was naturally flushed and vibrant. He beamed like a schoolboy as he took it all in.

"It's beautiful," he said, laughing in spite of himself. "It's so beautiful."

Faith laughed, too.

In the distance, a patch of blue grew out of the dark background of space. Elijah watched in wonder as it grew bigger. The pod bobbed again. Elijah looked around to find the pod was in water. The blue patch had widened into a perfect sapphire sky. The pod was at sea. He had to be hallucinating.

Elijah heard voices. Faint at first. The pod was silent. Janet had not spoken. He heard it again.

"Welcome home, Elijah."

A masculine voice.

"Welcome home, Elijah."

Now feminine, someone old. Soon several voices said it at once, then a chorus of hundreds, then thousands.

Behind Faith, one of the praying women said aloud: "Welcome home, Elijah." Faith ran back to the living room. Another one said it, then another. She returned to the bedroom and looked out into space. She watched the stars and listened as the praying women all fell into the same soft chant of "Welcome home, Elijah."

The pod pushed through the water into a dock of polished wood and stone, surrounded by a lush garden of delights. Elijah listened to the voices welcome him home. He sat relaxed in his chair, reclining as though asleep, but still he saw the wonders.

"It's all right now," he said.

Waiting on the dock was Clarence, the man in the pea coat. Next to him was his mother. At her legs stood the little girl he'd seen at the party, waving at him and smiling. Gathered around them were hundreds of others. Some looked familiar. Maybe he knew them as children or saw their faces in old photos taken before his time. They were all his people, just as he was theirs.

Faith gently shushed the praying women. She went to them and by turn touched their feet, waking them from their trance. They stood and left the room. Faith was alone. She closed her eyes and felt his essence fade.

"Welcome home, Elijah," she said.

She sat in a chair, thinking of Elijah. She had seen him through his final journey. Now she wondered how long it would be before she would have the strength to stand again.

Clarence helped Elijah from the pod. Elijah beamed as his people reached out to him with hugs and pats. He looked away from the homecoming, back into the blue horizon that faded into the starry blackness he'd come from. Faith was back there somewhere. Her memory faded quickly. It would return when her time was near, but for now, he was in a different place.

An indicator light started to blink in the pod.

"Life signals no longer detected," Janet said. *"End sequence initiated. So let it be."*

The pod imploded and disintegrated into a thousand glowing fragments that floated into the cosmos until they were indistinguishable from the stars.

About the Author

James B. Christensen is a novelist, screenwriter, musician, husband, and father of twin daughters. He is the author of *Honeymoon Phase,* a supernatural romantic comedy, *The Vessel*, an occult horror thriller, and *October Nights*, the first in the ongoing anthology series. He lives in Omaha, Nebraska.

Visit jamesbchristensen.com to sign up for his monthly newsletter and stay informed of upcoming releases.